Kris Bock

Whispers in the Dark

Pig River Press

Cover Design by Rollin Thomas

Pig River Press
Socorro, New Mexico

Copyright © 2011 by Chris Eboch
ISBN: 0615582230
ISBN-13: 978-0615582238

All rights reserved. For information about permission to reproduce selections from this book, contact the author through her website at www.krisbock.com.

This is a work of fiction. Names, characters, places, and incidents are the product of the author's imagination. Any resemblance to actual persons, living or dead, is entirely coincidental.

Whispers in the Dark

One

What had I gotten myself into?

I closed my eyes. Yes, I was driving, but a moment of distraction seemed safe enough, since I hadn't seen another car in half an hour. Even the jackrabbits and rattlesnakes were hiding in the shade, leaving the road clear of everything but rocks and ruts.

I was starting an adventure. I had to remind myself of that—an adventure. I wanted to be here. I wanted to get away from the city, the classroom and office, the people. You couldn't get much farther away than this, a tiny cluster of seven-hundred-year-old ruins in the Four Corners area of the Southwest. I had found the middle of nowhere.

As I had wanted, I reminded myself.

The car bumped into a pothole and my head smacked back on the headrest. Maybe I needed to pay more attention to the road after all. I had almost gotten used to the constant vibration from the rough dirt track, but I still got an occasional surprise from potholes as big as wading pools and ridges the size of speed bumps.

The vast landscape drew my attention, the open space leaving me a bit breathless, a reverse of claustrophobia. At a glance the scene lacked color, a wash of parched tan that spoke of emptiness, drought, death. I clenched the steering wheel and breathed deeply through my nose to filter out the dust pouring through the open window. I'd shut off the air-conditioning hours ago to keep my wreck from overheating.

It wasn't like I'd have to live in this dusty wasteland forever. I wanted to test myself in unfamiliar terrain, face life head-on, and prove I had healed. Then I could go back to normal life, stronger and ready to face more ordinary challenges. I didn't have to love it here; I only had to survive.

But my eyes, adapted to New England's green trees and grass, slowly started to appreciate this different palette. A painter probably could have named a dozen shades of brown, along with the soft reds—gentle shades of pink and orange and rust and purple—from the sandstone mesas. The scant vegetation added muted, dusty green. The rare patch of yellow wildflowers looked shockingly bright. And above it all lay the vast sky, incredibly blue and so bright it hurt my eyes to look up, even with sunglasses.

I gave a low whistle. "You're not in Boston anymore."

I saw a bump on the horizon, a tan cube that stood out against the undulating mesas only because of its straight lines and sharp angles. I took a quick breath and felt my heart rate speed. Almost there. I turned on the car radio, hoping for some distraction. The "seek" button scanned for five seconds before finally settling on a crackly voice. It sounded like a news program, something on tourists being careful about carjackings.

I had to smile. This, a bad neighborhood? Maybe for the mice.

I glanced around at the empty landscape. A black speck in the distant sky caught my eye, a hawk soaring in lazy circles. I shivered. I knew what it was like to be the mouse, helpless in a predator's claws.

But not here. I refused to be the mouse out here.

I tossed my head to shake away the thoughts. I was an adult, twenty-four years old, very nearly a professional woman. I had survived two years living in one of the rougher parts of Boston—I ruthlessly pushed down the worst of the memories—so I could certainly handle a few months in the desert.

I blamed the churning in my stomach on the spicy food from lunch and turned up the short drive to the visitors center.

I had my choice of a dozen empty parking spots. I only saw one other vehicle, an aging pickup pulled around the side of the building. I spent a minute brushing my hair and pulling it into a ponytail, then slathered on lip balm. A glance in the rearview mirror told me that nothing but a long shower would make up for the dust and sweat turning my brown hair muddy against skin a little too pink from the short hike I'd taken as a break from the drive the day before.

I wasn't likely to get a shower for a while, but fortunately people expected archaeologists to look grungy. Maybe today I'd avoid the raised eyebrows because I looked too young to be a real archaeologist.

I couldn't think of another excuse for dawdling, so I took a deep breath and stepped from the car.

The heat hit me like a physical blow. I'd heard an earlier weather report of 94 degrees, but my mind hadn't quite grasped the number. Sure, it was a dry heat—like an oven. I swayed for a moment and the building in front of me seemed to shimmer. I shook my head and crossed the few paces to the door. I hesitated on the threshold, my hand on the door handle. The building wasn't much bigger than my apartment back in Boston, so why did I feel like I was entering a portal to another dimension?

Maybe because I was entering a different world.

"You wanted this," I muttered. "Now take it and make it yours."

I drew in a deep breath, stretched up to my full five feet two inches, ignored my racing pulse, and pushed open the door.

I took off my sunglasses and blinked as my eyes adjusted to the dim interior. Two steps in, a counter cut the room in half. A closed door behind the counter suggested a back room. A man stood behind the counter, tall, stocky, and with a bit of a paunch.

He looked like a park ranger should, with brown hair and a bushy beard. He belonged in an Alaskan rainforest, though. He would look more at home in flannel than the green T-shirt he wore.

He smiled briefly, but his gaze dropped to the counter and he didn't speak.

I stepped forward. "Hello. I'm Kiley Hafford, the archaeologist." I didn't bother to add "student." After my work here allowed me to finish my master's thesis, I could claim the title, so why not start practicing now?

His gaze shot up at me and then dropped again. "You—you're early."

"Yes. I gave myself a week to drive from Boston, but things went so well it only took five days."

He didn't answer, merely glanced around as if searching for help.

Would this be a bigger deal than I'd expected? I clenched my jaw to keep from apologizing. When he looked at me again I forced myself to smile and said, "I hope it's not a problem."

"N-n-no. It's fine. I'm—I'm J-Jerry."

My mouth dropped open at his terrible stutter. Fortunately, he was staring down at his hands so he didn't see my surprise. No wonder he seemed so shy and nervous. I had to admire his courage for even taking a job like this, which put him in constant contact with tourists.

I held out my hand and said warmly, "I'm pleased to meet you."

He shook my hand and gave me a shy smile. "W-what do you want to do first?"

I glanced at my watch. Five o'clock. "I have time to look around the site before it gets dark, don't I? And you have a camping spot for me?" When he nodded to the questions, I added, "I wouldn't mind cleaning up a bit. There's water at the campground, right?" I realized I was asking only yes or no questions to take the pressure off him. I hoped he didn't notice and think I was being condescending.

"Yes, but—" He waved me around the counter and opened the door. I went through to a small room with a sofa, card table, miniature refrigerator, and stacks of boxes. Jerry pointed to another door and I found a tiny bathroom.

When I'd finished freshening up, I joined Jerry back at the counter. He gave me a tourist trail guide to the monument and pointed out the ruins where I'd be working. He also gave me a pass to campsite 12 and let me know with a few words and some hand gestures that it was the best, large and set away from the others.

"You're sure you want to stay there?" he stuttered.

"Yes. I like camping, and it doesn't make sense to commute out here every day." Besides, it would be a lot cheaper than paying for a hotel room every night and gas for the drive every day. "You don't mind if I stick a few things in your fridge once in a while, do you?"

He shook his head and smiled, a blush touching his cheeks above his dark beard.

"Will you be able to show me around tomorrow, if I need any help?"

Jerry shook his head again, "D-d-danesh will do that."

I suppressed a sigh. Jerry was all right, but who was this Danesh, if I'd heard the name right? What kind of name was it, anyway—male or female? I hoped for a woman but it seemed weird to ask.

"B-be careful at night," Jerry said. "St-stay in camp."

I frowned. "Why?" When he didn't answer, I asked, "Are there wild animals to worry about?"

It took him some time to get out the word no, and add, "Just safer." Again he seemed to search the room for help. I didn't want to force him to talk, so I said, "All right, I'll be careful." Probably they were used to tourists getting lost or something.

I thanked Jerry and headed for my car. Overall, I thought I'd handled the encounter fairly well. I thought I'd come across as friendly and confident, in charge even. And if my pulse was still jumping, no one could tell.

I drove the short distance to the campground and found space 12. Only a few other spaces were full; obviously this site didn't get the crowds of Chaco Canyon or Mesa Verde. All the better for me. Each site had a picnic table and a flat spot for a tent, surrounded by low scrub and trees. The campground even had a bathroom with flush toilets and sinks, but no showers. A pump outside the bathroom provided drinking water.

I put up my tent, a bright blue nylon dome supported by flexible metal poles. I tossed my sleeping bag and pad inside to help weight the tent against wind. Then I remembered the radio warning about thefts. Should I lock everything in my car when I was away from the campground? Taking the tent down and putting it up each day would be inconvenient, though, and maybe encourage someone to break into the car.

Surely crime wasn't a problem out here. The radio was probably talking about spots in town, like museum parking lots. I'd have to ask Jerry in the morning, or the mysterious Danesh. Until then, I'd take my chances.

My watch said 5:40, and the sun was well above the horizon. I had enough time for a hike around the canyon. The map said the Towers Loop was only a mile long. I changed from shorts into sturdy tan pants, for protection against ticks and sharp brush, and tucked the cuffs into my hiking boots. I grabbed the map and filled a bottle of water, then started walking.

On my way out of the campground, I passed a small RV behind a sign that said "Hosts." An old couple sat at the picnic table beside it. The man stayed bent over his newspaper, but the woman looked up, and I waved. She waved back and called out in a surprisingly low, gravelly voice, "You going to the ruins now? Don't be out too long. Once it gets

Whispers in the Dark

dark, you could get lost or twist your ankle."

"I'll be careful." I kept moving, not wanting to get stuck in a conversation. I figured I had several hours of daylight. I hadn't taken the time to properly outfit a backpack with a first aid kit and flashlight, but I was only planning to do a short walk on a trail designed for elderly tourists like those two.

I hurried along the trail until I reached the canyon rim, where I stopped and grinned. The canyon cut across the land in front of me—maybe more of a ravine, really, several miles long but only a quarter-mile across and a few hundred feet deep. The bottom looked shady and cool, while the sun lit up the small ruin to my right.

The now-roofless structure wouldn't impress anyone but an archaeologist—except for the way it perched recklessly atop a thirty-foot boulder. The boulder sloped at a sharp angle, so it looked like the whole structure should slide into the canyon. And it had been there for over 700 years! I skimmed the pamphlet and confirmed what I remembered: Stronghold House was part of a large pueblo that once filled the canyon slope below. Ironically, the lower floors built down in the canyon had crumbled and been washed away, so now only the top story remained, safe on the enormous boulder.

I spotted carved hand and toeholds in the rock, leading up to the low doorway. I tried to imagine the Anasazi living there centuries before, scrambling up the steep side of the boulder as easily as I walked up the stairs to my second-floor apartment. I half-closed my eyes to blur my vision and tried to picture the way it must have been before the walls crumbled and the roof collapsed. I imagined small, tanned people in loincloths, women on the roof, crouched over their work, children playing nearby, men returning from hunting or working their cultivated fields. I could almost hear their cheerful shouts.

I opened my eyes and turned down the path along the canyon rim, humming with pleasure.

The next structure, which was called Falling House, looked even less accessible. It clung to a rugged outcropping of rock separated from the canyon rim by a five-foot crevasse, as if a piece of the canyon wall had peeled away but stopped short of falling. Several ruined walls still stood, the jagged line of their crumbled tops silhouetted against the blue sky. A diagram in the pamphlet showed several rooms and a round kiva or ceremonial room.

I couldn't wait to explore further. Of course, regular tourists weren't allowed to leave the trail, but one of the perks of being an archaeologist was special access. For the next few weeks, this would be my playground.

The next site on the map was a vandalized rock shelter, and the trail guide complained that people had torn down the walls before it could be excavated. Only part of one wall and a jumble of stones remained. But the guide also mentioned that the site might have yielded storage jars or food remains, had it been left for archaeologists. Since my interest was ancient food, I decided to creep down for a closer look.

I moved carefully, so as not to disturb the loose rocks, and squatted near the biggest pile of rubble. I gently lifted a few broken pieces, putting them back in exactly the same place after I'd examined them. I couldn't do much with the fragments, but as always, I marveled over touching something from the ancient past.

Tomorrow would be soon enough for scientific method, for testing and hypothesizing. Tonight I only wanted to touch the magic of this ancient world. I closed my eyes and tried to feel some ancient presence, to hear whispers from the past.

The air seemed to tremble with possibilities. If only I believed in magic—

A shout slashed the air. I twisted so fast I tumbled onto my backside.

I gaped up at the man towering over me. Bare chest, muscular and bronzed. Black hair pulled back from a face full of sharp planes and angles. Dark eyes fierce under scowling brows.

My heart jolted painfully. I'd come face to face with an ancient warrior. He was gorgeous.

And furious.

At me.

Two

"Don't you read signs?"

I blinked at the apparition. "Uh ..."

He gestured back at the main path. "The signs at every turn saying 'Stay on the path'? The notice at the entrance telling you to leave artifacts alone? I could have you arrested and fined."

Oh. I felt color flooding my cheeks. My pounding heart refused to slow yet, and the rush of adrenaline turned my arms and legs to jelly, but I rose steadily enough. I tried to ignore the heat in my face and the queasy feeling of panic in my stomach, which hadn't yet accepted the message that I wasn't in danger.

"I'm Kylie Hafford," I said. "The archaeologist. Are you Danesh?"

I saw a satisfying flash of surprise and then guilt. Or maybe I had merely imagined it, as his face settled immediately into a neutral mask. "Yes, I'm Danesh." He hesitated before adding, "It's nice to meet you."

"The pleasure's all mine."

He must have caught my irony, because he almost smiled—I think. He said, "I'm sorry I startled you. I wasn't expecting you yet, and ..." He shrugged. "I've been noticing scuff marks in the ground, off the trail where tourists aren't supposed to go. I figured someone was poking around, maybe looking for treasure."

"And you assumed I was your treasure hunter?"

His gaze narrowed on my face, and I had to stop myself from backing away. He said, "Maybe you do have a right to look around, but it's still a problem.

If tourists see you down here, they'll think they can do it, too. They'll pick things up, move them around, take them home. Even if they bring their finds to us in the visitors center—and they do that all the time—it forever ruins our chance of finding an artifact in its proper place, maybe learning more—"

"I know that," I snapped. "They do teach us a thing or two in archaeology classes." I stepped up to the path so he wasn't looking down at me. He barely backed up, so I had to pass within arm's reach of him, but I felt steadier once we were on the same level and I realized he wasn't that tall. Well, everyone was tall compared to me. But he only had half a foot on me, so the towering effect had been a result of our respective positions and his scowl.

I stood as tall as I could and put my hands on my hips. "So what do you expect me to do, study this place through binoculars?"

Once again his smile vanished before I was sure I'd seen it. "We can do better than that. We'll get you a uniform shirt so you look more official and a sign to put on the trail that says 'Archaeologist at work.' If you see anyone watching you, let them know what you're doing and why, and that you have permission, but they don't." The half-smile hovered a second longer this time. "You could say it a little nicer than that, I suppose."

I could probably say anything nicer than this guy, but I decided I'd start by not mentioning that. "Great. When can I get a shirt?"

He glanced over his shoulder toward the sun. That gave me a chance to drop my gaze from his face and notice that he was wearing running shorts and trail-runner shoes, with a T-shirt tucked into his waistband. He must've been jogging. That explained the bare chest and the glistening sweat, now vanishing in the dry air. I wished he'd put his shirt back on. All that bare skin was really distracting. If I dressed like that, I'd be accused of acting like a slut and have to put up with whistles and stares, but men—

He turned back and I jerked my gaze to his face. "How about first thing tomorrow," he said. "Jerry's waiting for me and I'm already late. Come by the office a little before eight o'clock and have some coffee."

Now that was the nicest thing he'd said yet. But before I could answer, he said, "I'll walk you back to the campground."

"That's not necessary. I'll make sure I leave no trace and move along. You go on ahead so you don't keep Jerry waiting."

We locked gazes. I felt like I'd gotten into some battle of wills, and I didn't even know why. But Danesh obviously thought he owned this place and everything in it. If I didn't stake my claim now, it would be that much harder later. I felt my heart thump five, six, seven times and refused to move anything. Not even my eyes. He'd get no placating smiles or soft feminine pleading from me.

Finally he said, "All right. Be careful. You have a couple of hours of light, but it gets dark quickly and the temperature drops fast. Snakes come out at dusk, and it's pitch black out here after dark unless the moon is out."

I resisted the urge to roll my eyes. "I'll be careful."

He looked like he wanted to say more, but he turned and jogged up the path. I watched him for a minute, admiring the way the evening sun bronzed his back as the muscles rippled. Too bad his personality was as hard and tough as his body.

I sighed. It was just as well that I didn't like Danesh. He was probably used to giggling tourists and adoring local girls. I'd made enough of a fool of myself without getting tongue-tied over his mouthwatering good looks. He didn't know it, but he'd given me a test—a hard one. My hand trembled only a little as I retrieved my water bottle, so I convinced myself I had passed so far. One day, I would convince my body to stop panicking at the slightest surprise. For now, I had to promise myself it would get better. Each time I faced my fears, I got a little stronger. I might not be back to normal yet, but I could see normal from here.

I decided to finish hiking the loop, but I stayed on the main path. Much as I hated being lectured, Danesh had a point. I should set a good example for the few tourists still out.

Two middle-aged men stood at a viewpoint looking across the canyon through binoculars. I paused behind them and tried to read the sign from three feet away. It said Pueblo Storehouses and had a sketch of the far canyon wall, with the storehouses outlined in red. That was one place I'd look for seed samples. I squinted, but with the shadows in the canyon I couldn't make out anything on the far wall.

One of the men lowered his binoculars and turned to me. "We can't find them. Do you want to try?"

I hesitated, but the men looked harmless enough, both about fifty and wearing polo shirts, one blue and one green, with shorts. I tried to search my instincts for any sign of danger and found none, besides the usual background anxiety. The man in blue handed me the binoculars and backed away to give me room. I smiled, remembering my comment to Danesh about studying through binoculars.

I studied the diagram and then focused the binoculars on the canyon wall, below the far rim where I had already hiked on my way over.

The man said, "It looks like the sandstone, I think."

I scanned across the canyon wall and finally spotted formations that didn't look natural. "I see them. The walls are rounded so they don't stand out that well, but you can see a rectangular doorway." I tried to focus the binoculars better. Something looked odd on one of the walls, like a large stone that wasn't quite the right color. I couldn't figure it out, but no doubt it would make sense when I explored more closely. Or had the storehouses been damaged? Maybe even recently, by someone leaving the path to look for treasure? If I found anything strange, I'd have to let Danesh know.

I grimaced at the thought. Maybe I'd tell Jerry instead.

I handed the binoculars back to the man and tried to explain where the storehouses were. I realized I'd been hearing a strange sound, a low rumbling. I glanced around, unable to tell the source. Surely not thunder, as the skies remained a clear, deep blue.

"Sounds like a plane," the man in green said. The two had lowered their binoculars and were holding hands. I felt myself relax a notch.

We all scanned the sky as the sound grew louder. He had to be right about a plane, but it was creepy to hear that sound and not be able to see any source. I guess sound traveled far with no city noise to mute it.

Finally I spotted a small, black plane, surprisingly low in the air. It seemed to be coming straight toward us.

"I wonder why they're so low," Green said.

"Tourists who want a close look at the canyon?" I suggested.

"There aren't any official tour flights. We checked. Could be a private pilot seeing the sights."

The plane veered sharply to the left, leaving a trail of white across the sky.

"But they're heading away now," Green said. "I hope they're not in trouble. With all the mesas and mountains around here, I'd want a little more altitude."

I imagined flying only a few hundred feet above the ground. Would it be comforting to have your landing so visible, or terrifying because one slip could have you slamming into the ground? "They'd call someone if they were in trouble, wouldn't they? They must have a radio."

"They should have a radio, but they'd have a better chance of reaching someone higher up, where the signal won't be blocked by the peaks. This low, they're flying under the radar. They won't even show up on the government's tracking system, so if they go down, searchers won't know where."

Funny, I knew the phrase "flying under the radar," but I'd never thought of it quite so literally. Blue gave Green a playful shoulder bump. "It's probably nothing. Tom's a worrier. He likes to make up dire scenarios for random strangers."

Tom laughed. "One of these days I'll be right."

I chuckled with them, then thanked the men for the use of the binoculars and moved on. But I kept glancing in the direction the plane had gone, watching for smoke or any other sign of trouble. No doubt I just had my city instincts on alert in this unfamiliar territory, but I couldn't help imagining what would happen to the victims of a plane crash out in the desert or on one of the peaks. I saw nothing more of the plane, though, so I had to trust they were all right.

I finished the loop well before dark, cleaned up in the restroom, and sat at my picnic table to eat the second half of the sandwich I'd been keeping in a cooler since lunch. The block of dry ice would keep my yogurt and cheese sticks cool for a couple more days. Then I'd be stuck with dried and canned food until I made a trip into town, something I didn't relish given that my compact car obviously wasn't designed for the rough roads. Well, I hadn't expected luxury.

I had expected quiet, though. Yet the night filled with sounds as dusk fell. Birds, insects, and rustling in the dark. I strained my ears and tried to identify the sounds. Bird calls were easy enough. That low buzz had to be some kind of insect, and I convinced myself it was only creepy because I wasn't used to it. Rustling in the bushes was harder to dismiss. I forced myself to breathe deeply and repeated in my mind, *Just animals. Only animals. You're safe here.*

A squirrel scurried up a tree nearby, proving my point, and I let out a burst of nervous laughter.

I went back to my deep breathing. I didn't want

to crawl into my tent until I felt comfortable there, or I knew I'd spend the night imagining monsters sneaking around the thin protection of my nylon walls. I could sleep in my car, as I had done several times on the drive out, when I wasn't sure of my security. But this campground would be my home for weeks. I had to get used to it, face my fears until they disappeared. I closed my eyes and concentrated on the cool air on my skin, the soft breeze.

I heard voices in the distance and a thump like something being dropped. I told myself it was good to know others were within hailing distance. I breathed, and listened, and finally felt my heart slow and my muscles relax. I thought I might be able to sleep.

A new sound drifted through the air, and my breath caught in my throat. I heard a soft sobbing, like a woman crying.

Should I check it out, see if someone needed help? But no one was calling for help, and I couldn't target the sound.

It was probably some animal or bird, but still, I felt goosebumps prickle my skin. I went to my car for a sweater, trying to blame the drop in temperature for my chills.

When I opened the car door, the overhead light came on, shockingly bright. I jumped and glanced around, feeling oddly guilty, as if I'd insulted the night. I grabbed my sweater, closed the door quickly, and stood for a minute waiting for my eyes to readjust as the darkness pressed around me.

The crying seemed to ripple in the air, coming from nowhere and everywhere.

And then it faded, leaving only the echo of its memory in the dark, and a great sadness.

Three

I woke and stared at the bright blue nylon above me, wondering where I was. Then I remembered—away from it all. Yeah, right. I'd expected to have challenges; that was the whole point. But being in the middle of nowhere had already held a few surprises.

My face felt chilly in the cool morning air. I'd read about the possible 40-degree temperature swings between night and day, but I hadn't quite believed it. I wriggled into a sweatshirt and jeans and bolted for the restroom. Washing my hands and face in cold water didn't warm me up, so I decided to jog to the canyon rim and get my blood pumping.

By the time I'd done the quarter-mile, I was gasping. I'd managed the Boston Marathon less than a year earlier, but I hadn't jogged in six months. Maybe here, at last, I could try again. If I got back into the habit in totally unfamiliar surroundings, maybe I'd be able to jog in Boston again. Or wherever I went next.

I stopped at the edge of the canyon to catch my breath. I had the place to myself, with no one in sight except the birds and squirrels. The ruins along the rim glowed golden as the sunrise spread across the desert floor. I shaded my eyes and looked down into the canyon, where vegetation grew lush and green along a small river. A great place to spend a hot afternoon, but for now I preferred to stand in the sun.

I strolled along the rim trail, admiring the view. To the southeast, the desert stretched out flat for miles and then suddenly jutted up into a mountain range at the far horizon. I couldn't even guess at the distance, since I wasn't used to seeing more than a few hundred feet in any direction. Even the field camps I'd joined had been in wooded areas. Maybe I should have felt exposed in the Southwest's wide-open spaces. Yet somehow everything combined to feel cozy: the small canyon, slightly over a mile long; the dozen ruins along the canyon rim, most no bigger than my apartment; the friendly tourists who felt the lure of this place.

I tried to imagine living here in ancient times, knowing nothing else but this landscape and the few hundred people in my community. That abstract concept was starting to feel more real, even appealing.

I shivered as I lost the heat from my run. I turned and jogged back toward the campground, my lungs burning. At least fighting for breath and watching my footing kept my mind almost too busy for other thoughts. Though I glanced nervously at the bushes, I avoided full-fledged panic.

I heard a distant car door slam. As I reached the campground, the restroom door swung shut. I had once again entered the modern world of humans. I slowed to a walk and enjoyed the chirping of birds in the trees above, the sounds of a lazy world waking.

A man's voice broke the peace. I couldn't catch the words but the harsh tone stopped me in my tracks. A woman's voice, high-pitched and anxious, struggled to compete.

And then a crack, like a branch breaking or a single clap of hands, cut off the voices.

I stood trembling, my stomach in knots. Part of my mind screamed *Run!* but I couldn't turn away. My fingernails dug into the palms of my hands. My shallow breath rasped in my ears.

A man burst out of the trees, barreling toward me. I stumbled back, but my legs felt so shaky I couldn't escape. I made some wordless noise as he brushed past me muttering curses, but I'm not sure he noticed me at all. I watched until he disappeared up the path.

I hugged myself, chilled again. I turned and spotted the old woman at the host site. She stood on the steps to her RV, looking after the man and shaking her head. Then she came down the steps and crossed to the path. She raised a hand briefly in greeting.

I stared at her. "Should we …"

"I'll take care of it." She headed further into the campground. She was heavyset, but moved quickly and quietly. She disappeared among the trees and I stood still as the seconds slipped past. I should go after the woman, see if someone needed help. I should keep an eye on the man, see where he went, find out what he was doing. I should go about my business and pretend nothing had happened. I should go for help.

For the life of me, I couldn't decide.

I took a deep breath and blew it out. I wasn't here to hide from trouble. I had to know what happened. I would find out and then decide what to do next. I took a step in the direction the old woman had gone.

A voice called out behind me. I spun with a hand to my thudding chest.

The sun streamed into my eyes, half blinding me. I could only make out a dark figure striding toward me. I stepped back and stumbled over some rock or stick. I struggled for balance.

The figure closed the distance between us in a heartbeat. I gasped as hands grabbed my arms with bruising force.

"What is it? What's wrong?"

At least now I recognized the dark, frowning face. I couldn't speak, could only struggle for breath and try to fight back the panic.

"You're white as a ghost," Danesh said. "Are you sick?"

I shook my head. He slipped an arm around me and held me tight against his side. "You'd better sit down." I couldn't have broken his grip, so I had no choice but to let him lead me to my campsite. He had to feel my trembling. I hated that he had seen me like that. I hated the panic that could freeze me in an instant, shatter my peace of mind, and turn me into someone I barely recognized. I hated losing control of my own body, feeling—no, knowing—that I was helpless and weak.

By the time we reached my picnic table, the anger had steadied me. I tried to shrug off his arm and grumbled, "I'm all right."

He let go of me but hovered close until I sat. I clenched my hands in my lap and willed myself to stop shaking.

"Tell me what happened," he demanded.

I thought about what I'd witnessed. I wasn't sure what had happened, but if my guess was right, the women wouldn't want a man interrupting now. "It's nothing. I just got a little lightheaded. Too much exercise on an empty stomach."

He crouched beside me and looked into my face. I managed a smile.

He looked very serious. "I should have brought the doughnuts."

"What?" I gaped at him.

He grinned, a sudden flash that transformed his face and vanished so quickly I wasn't sure I'd really seen it. "I was looking for you to invite you in for coffee and doughnuts. But you'd better not wait. You have some food here, right? Tell me where and I'll get it."

No doubt he meant well, but I had to take control. "I'll get it." I tore my gaze away from his face and stood. I even managed not to jump when he shot to his feet beside me and put a hand on my elbow. I pulled away from the steadying hand and strode to my car. I really felt too queasy to want food, but I'd made the excuse and I had to stick with it. I found a granola bar and choked down a few bites. I smiled at him. "Much better."

He studied my face like he could read my whole history in it. I withstood it for a few seconds, then turned back to my car and found a water bottle. I took a drink and another bite of the granola bar without looking at him.

"Maybe you should drive over to the visitors center."

"I'm not an invalid," I snapped. "It's not even half a mile."

His lips twitched. "I guess you are feeling better. All right, ready to go?"

I nodded. I wasn't, but I was too drained to think of a good excuse. Besides, sitting at my campsite brooding over my cowardly display would not get the day off to a better start. I prayed he wouldn't insist on holding my arm the whole way.

He stayed close but did not touch me again.

At the visitors center, Danesh unlocked the door and swung it wide. The door creaked, and Jerry, standing behind the counter, jumped. His hand hit the phone, the handset clattered onto the counter, and he fumbled to replace it, his face going red above his beard.

Danesh crossed the room without a glance in Jerry's direction. He called over his shoulder to me, "We're not open yet. Come into the back."

I ignored his command and smiled at Jerry. "Good morning Jerry! How are you?" He gave me one swift glance then looked down as he stammered a reply. I realized my greeting had been excessively warm, more for Danesh's sake than Jerry's. No doubt everyone ignored chubby, stuttering Jerry when the hot young warrior was around. And no doubt Danesh bossed Jerry like he bossed everyone else. I'd let Danesh see he wasn't everyone's favorite.

Jerry's gaze jerked around the small office, avoiding my eyes. I realized I was making him uncomfortable, so I gave him another smile he probably didn't see and went into the back room. Jerry came in behind me. Danesh handed him a mug and asked me, "Anything in it?"

I noticed he had two more mugs of coffee already poured. Just to be contrary, I said, "Actually, I'd prefer tea."

"All right." He grabbed a fresh mug, filled it with water, and stuck it in the microwave.

I picked a doughnut and sat on the couch next to Jerry. Danesh fixed my tea and then sat cross-legged on the floor. He studied me without expression, and I felt my face heating. I tried to think of something to say, but my mind was painfully empty. I took a sip of tea and nearly burned my throat.

Finally Danesh said, "Tell us about your work."

That seemed safe enough, so I launched into an explanation of grain and seed analysis. If I found food residue, I could determine its genetic makeup, then hopefully draw some conclusions about when the Ancestral Pueblo People had domesticated various plants and what those plants were like at the time. I planned to focus on the storehouses, but given time I'd take samples in other areas as well.

When I wound down, Danesh said, "I notice you're careful to call them the Ancestral Pueblo People, and not the Anasazi. That name seems to stick, even though it's inappropriate."

"I know, it means 'ancient enemies' in Navaho, and it's insulting to the ancient people's descendants, who are not Navaho." I was glad I hadn't given him another chance to lecture. "I suppose you're especially sensitive."

He gave the almost-smile that seemed to be his trademark. "That's me, Mr. Sensitive."

Could he actually be poking fun at himself? More likely he was teasing me. "I just mean, if you're ..." I trailed off. I didn't really know what he was or what might offend him. He didn't look Navaho; his face had too many sharp angles, with high cheekbones and deep-set eyes. But that didn't mean he was Puebloan, and I was no expert in native tribes.

He said, "If you mean genetically, I'm half Filipino and half Danish, with a lot of Spanish on the Filipino side. And if you mean professionally, I'm a park ranger but my background is biology, not anthropology or archaeology."

I stared at him. Filipino and Danish combined to make this? Wasn't genetics amazing!

I wasn't sure where to go from there, so I turned to Jerry. "What about you? How long have you worked here?"

I only half listened, my mind still trying to make sense of Danesh. I felt like he'd caught me at something. But he had to know people would make the wrong assumption, especially seeing him here, where everyone was focused on native history. If he didn't want people to think he was Native American, he should have gotten a job at Carlsbad Caverns or Crater Lake.

He probably did it on purpose. Maybe he liked the extra glamour of playing native to the tourists. Maybe he liked to see people squirm when he told them the truth. I had a feeling he was still staring at me, but I refused to check. If he meant to be unnerving, he was certainly good at it.

I caught the end of Jerry's question. "The campground? Oh yes, it's fine."

"Did you have a quiet night?" Danesh asked.

"What?"

"Did you have a quiet night. No strange lights, sounds, manifestations?"

I stared at him. What was he suggesting? The crying sound had been strange, even creepy, but that didn't make it supernatural. Maybe he was trying to trick me into saying something stupid.

Danesh gazed back with a completely serious expression, but then Jerry broke the mood by giggling. "G-g-ghosts!"

Four

"What on earth are you two talking about?" I demanded.

Danesh smiled, and this time the smile lingered. I almost gasped—It was like the sun coming up. He said, "We've been hearing stories from the tourists. Floating lights in the canyon, voices coming from the ruins at night, even a strange smell—what did they insist it was?"

"B-burning sage."

"Marijuana, more likely. We'll get a rash of reports like this once in awhile. Some tourist sees another tourist walking with a flashlight across the canyon and jumps to supernatural conclusions. Then the rumors start, and next thing you know we'll have a coven of crystal worshippers wanting to hold midnight rituals in The Castle and commune with the ancient dead."

"What do you do?" I couldn't stop staring at Danesh's smile, as if I had to drink it in before it disappeared again.

"Make them hold their rituals in the parking lot. Tell them it was the site of a major kiva, if that will keep them happy. We can't have a bunch of impressionable flakes mass hallucinating in a dark, rubble-strewn canyon. A few always sneak off, and we get at least one sprained ankle. On the bright side, it's the most entertainment we ever get around here."

Jerry only stuttered a little as he said, "They always want Danesh to join them. Think he's a shaman or something."

I looked at Danesh and raised my eyebrows. "And you disillusion them?"

He didn't answer, but his smile faded. I hated to see it go.

The silence stretched out. Had I said something wrong? If so, I had no idea what. Whoever said women were the moody half of the population was an idiot. Well, I refused to feel stupid for no reason. I scrambled for another topic. "The woman at the host site seems nice."

Danesh gave that brief almost-smile that now looked so dim in comparison to the real thing. "Did she get your entire life history out of you yet?"

"No, we've barely spoken."

"She's behind schedule. Usually it doesn't take her more than five minutes to learn everything about a newcomer." He looked at Jerry, inviting him to share the amusement, but Jerry merely mumbled something and headed for the other room. At least he wasn't willing to make fun of a sweet old woman.

I said, "It sounds like she's doing a great job, then," even though I didn't like the idea of having to dodge her questions myself.

"Yeah, she's a real mama tiger," Danesh said. "It's just as well, since we've been getting some complaints lately."

I thought of the angry man. "What kind of complaints?"

"Things missing from cars and campsites. Food, mostly, but also some camping gear. One guy insisted bears got into his cooler, but we've never seen a bear around here." He shrugged. "Nothing too serious. Half the people probably forgot to pack something. And when the wind picks up, you'd be surprised at what it can blow away. But if you want to be extra safe, lock everything in your car and park your car over here during the day."

It was like being back in the city! "You aren't very trusting, are you?"

"Maybe not. But then, neither are you."

Before I could think of an answer, he rose fluidly

and said, "More tea?" When I shook my head, he added, "Then we might as well get started." He gathered the mugs and started washing them.

We? Great. "I don't really need a guide. I have a trail map and I'm sure I can find my way around."

"Ah, but I can tell you things you'll never find in a trail guide."

I made a face at his back. He was probably right, but I was in no mood for more lectures. No doubt they figured Danesh would be a better guide because of Jerry's stuttering, but I'd much rather listen to Jerry then feel awkward all day long. "I really don't want to hike this morning. I'd like to get started on my work while it's cool."

He turned and gave me a long, unreadable look. "Some other time, then."

"Yes." I managed a quick smile.

"Take a key to the office. Then you can get in here after hours if you need to get something from the fridge or use the phone. You might get cell reception out here, depending on your provider, but it can be inconsistent, especially during bad weather."

"Thanks." I took the key and headed into the other room.

I wanted to get out of there, but Jerry held up a hand to stop me and gestured to a pile of magazines and brochures on the counter. His stuttering seemed even worse, but I gathered he was offering me material on the area and its ancient people. Poor guy, he must stutter more when he was nervous, and for some reason he was trying hard to impress me.

I glanced through the information, but most of it was familiar. I'd read dozens of books and probably a hundred research papers on the Ancestral Pueblo People. Though my personal studies focused only on food, I needed a thorough understanding of my subjects. I didn't want to hurt his feelings, though, so I said, "Thank you! I'll take a couple of them back to my campsite now and leave the others here so they won't get dirty."

He stared at me with this strange pleading

look. His mouth opened and closed but nothing came out. I felt myself turning red in sympathetic embarrassment.

A sharp knock on the door made us both jump. Jerry hurried past me and opened it just enough to speak to whomever was on the other side. I didn't catch their words, but I assumed Jerry was saying the office wasn't open yet. I grabbed a few of the brochures at random, ready to get out of there.

When Jerry turned from the door, he was smiling. He said, "Your sign and—and shirt." I waited while he shuffled back to the counter and got them. He kept his hand on the shirt when I reached for it and asked if I was going to the storehouses. Hadn't I already said I wanted to start with the storehouses? I hoped he wasn't trying to flirt. He was a nice guy, but I wasn't interested.

I said, "I need to go get my gear, and then I'll probably be at the storehouses all morning." I almost added, "if anyone needs me," but who could possibly need me? If I was lucky, I wouldn't see anyone until I got back to the campground—after Danesh and Jerry had left for the day.

Jerry told me to have a great day and finally I escaped.

I turned toward the path to the campground, then hesitated. I knew you couldn't see the Pueblo storehouses from above, and the way down wasn't marked, since it wasn't open to tourists. Maybe I should find the way first, before too many tourists came out to see me stumbling around, and before Danesh decided he had to "help" me again. Then I could get my gear and set up quickly.

I gave a quick glance over my shoulder to make sure the men were still safely in the office, then strode toward the canyon rim. When I turned onto the rim trail, the trees hid me from view. I didn't see anyone along the canyon, either. I sighed and felt my shoulders unknot. If I could get a little peace and quiet, I could find my balance again. I could forget about the angry man, about Jerry's awkward flirting, about Danesh startling me and then bossing me around. I felt my face heat at the memory of how he'd caught me shaking and incoherent.

I shook my head hard. It didn't do any good to dwell on that. I shouldn't blame myself for feeling fragile sometimes, especially in a strange, new place with men yelling and rushing at me. The next time would be better. I simply had to act normal, and soon everything would be normal.

The path was bordered by a few feet of bushes and rocks at the edge of the rim, with an occasional railing to keep people back from the steepest drops. I slowed where I knew the storehouses had to be. A sign warned people to stay on the trail and I smiled, feeling deliciously naughty.

I edged off the path and leaned forward to see down into the canyon. The bottom looked far away. Standing a couple of feet back from the rim, I couldn't see the cliff on this side, so it might have been a straight drop. My stomach gave a flip, but I took a deep breath and fought back a slight feeling of vertigo. As soon as I took a step closer, I'd be able to see the way down, and it wouldn't be that steep—at least not where I was going down.

I heard a scuffling sound from below. Probably birds in the bushes or lizards coming out to enjoy the sun. I thought larger animals like foxes and skunks would have gone into hiding by this time of day. I crept a few feet along the rim, moving silently. Maybe I could get a look at the animal before it saw me and fled.

I heard a faint noise again. I was right above it. Squirrel? Robin? Something more exotic? I leaned forward to look over the rim.

A strange man popped up in front of me.

Five

I yelped and jerked back so hard I fell on my backside. I scrambled back, my heart thudding, until I backed into a rock and grunted with pain.

The man gasped. "I'm sorry! I'm sorry! I didn't mean to startle you." He scrambled over the rim.

The sharp pain to my lower back had snapped me out of my panic. It was a repeat of yesterday, me on my rear, a strange man standing over me. At least this one wasn't yelling or glaring at me. He held out his hand.

Mid-twenties, medium height, broad shoulders like an athlete. Short blond hair and a friendly, boyish face. He looked so concerned that I forced myself to take his hand and let him help me up. "Are you all right? Not hurt?" He didn't let go even once I was standing.

I pulled my hand away. "No." I brushed off my shorts. "This is getting to be a habit," I muttered.

"What?"

"Nothing." How many times would I have to feel foolish on this visit? What was it with these men, jumping out at you when you thought you were all alone? I glared at the guy. "What were you doing?"

He shrugged and gave a sheepish smile. "Just looking around."

"Didn't you see the sign that says 'Stay on Path'?" I gestured to it. "You can read, can't you? Do you think the rules don't apply—"

Great, I sounded like Danesh. Maybe this man had a perfectly legitimate reason for being off the path. Even if he didn't, I didn't have to treat him like a child.

I took a slow, deep breath. "Sorry. Too much adrenaline."

He nodded. "It's the flight-or-fight response. It has to come out somehow."

I studied him more closely. He had vivid green eyes and was more cute than handsome. He wore a button-up shirt and khaki pants, fairly dressy for this part of the country. He looked like someone I might have met at one of the bars around Harvard Square.

I gave a cool smile. "That's understanding of you. But really, we can't have people going off the path without permission." I made the statement almost a question. If he did have permission, I would apologize profusely—and strangle Danesh later for not warning me.

"I know. If everyone went wherever they wanted, they'd destroy the landscape, trample valuable artifacts, and generally make a mess of things." He glanced toward the office, though trees hid the building. "I'm going to have to throw myself on your mercy. I promise I didn't take anything. I just find it so fascinating out here. I've seen the storehouses from across the canyon, and I wanted a closer look, but those guys in the office are so ... uh ... they don't like to make exceptions."

"That's a diplomatic way of putting it. But what makes you think I'm any different?"

He winced. "Fair enough." He held out his hands, palms up and wrists together, as if waiting for the handcuffs. "I humbly surrender."

I had to smile. It was hard to stay mad at someone who accepted that you were totally right, and who kept a sense of humor about it. "I'll let you off with a warning this time, but only because I'm anxious to get to work. Promise me you'll stay on the path in the future, though."

"Absolutely. So you do work here?" He bent to pick up the sign I had dropped.

"Yes, at least temporarily. I'm doing some archaeological research."

"Hey, that's great! I'm something of an amateur archaeologist myself. Oh, don't worry—I don't go around picking up arrowheads or taking souvenir bricks. I just mean I'm interested. You sound like the perfect guide. I don't suppose you'd have time to show me around?"

He seemed nice enough, but I hadn't even started on my work. And I could hardly go traipsing off on a hike with this guy when I'd refused Danesh. I tried to think of a gracious refusal.

"I'm sorry," the man said. "I should introduce myself. I'm Sean."

"Kylie. Look, I'm flattered, but I really need to get to work."

"Of course. Maybe later? Do you have plans for lunch?"

"Uh, I was planning to picnic. I didn't notice a lot of choices."

He gave a knowing smile. "Ah, but that's where you're wrong. Some of the best food in the state can be found only a few miles from here. Joline's Diner, at the trading post."

"Kind of a long drive for lunch, isn't it?"

He shrugged. "Some people commute fifty, sixty miles to work every day. But there's never traffic, so it's not bad. And if you'd go that far just to work, what's fifteen miles for great food? Come on, give me a chance to make up for startling you." He gave me this cute grin, like a little boy trying to persuade Mom to buy candy. It was like he knew he could be charming, but he didn't take it seriously, so he came across as sweet rather than cocky.

I tried to tune into my instincts, but they were still jumping from two scares in as many hours. My instincts had been on overdrive for the last six months anyway, so I hardly trusted them. Still, I said, "I'm not in the habit of getting into a car with a stranger."

His smile widened. "And that's why we should go for a hike together first. Anyway, if you want, you can drive, or take a separate car."

"Look, I'll think about it. Maybe I'll run into you later."

"Fair enough. If you're around for long, I'm sure we'll run into each other again. I really would love to hear more about your work." He waved and headed down the path.

I watched him go with mixed feelings. Of course it was flattering to have a good-looking guy express interest, especially one who didn't mistake me for a 16-year-old at first. And I was trying to return to normal life, which would, one hoped, include dating. But I had to take it slow or risk a serious meltdown. I had enough stress at the moment.

I set up my sign on the rim and started down the off-limits side trail. It was a narrow, steep switchback but felt safe enough so long as I went slowly. I found the storehouses about halfway down the canyon wall. No wonder they were hard to spot from across the canyon unless you had binoculars. Wherever the Ancient Ones had found a cave-like depression in the rock, they had closed the front with blocks of the same color. At one time even the entrance holes would have been sealed with stones and mud to keep out mice and other animals. In the winter, the people could have broken the seals to retrieve their food and then closed up the storehouses again.

Now all the storehouses were open, and anything major, like pots or baskets, had been removed long ago. But I hoped to find a few seeds caught in cracks or a bit of dried vegetable matter stuck to some rock. I might not even be able to see material with my eyes, but I had a magnifying glass and I would take scrapings to study under a microscope.

I noticed some scuff marks in the dirt, including the imprint of athletic shoes with little suction cups on the bottom. I had noticed that Sean was wearing expensive athletic shoes, not what I would've chosen for hiking, but safe enough on most of the paths. I was still wearing tennis shoes myself. I followed the prints along the path. I couldn't see them constantly, but every once in a while a patch of little circles in the dust showed where he had gone. It looked like he had stayed on the trail, at least.

I suddenly realized that by asking me out, he'd totally deflected my anger. I'd never decided not to report him, but he'd walked away as if doing me a favor by not coming on too strong. Had that been his intent, to get out of trouble? Or was I reading far too much into things?

I shook my head. I'd grown so suspicious. Was it an excuse to avoid contact?

I had to start dating again sometime, unless I planned to be celibate for the rest of my life. I wanted a family someday. No hurry on that, but if I dismissed every man I met as somehow inappropriate, I'd never get back in the saddle, so to speak.

Maybe it made sense to go on a few casual dates out here, if only to test my reactions. The fact that I was only visiting gave me a kind of safety. If things got too intense, I had the perfect excuse to back away.

I shrugged. I'd probably never see Sean again, no matter how small the community. Danesh was too good-looking for my comfort, and his personality left a lot to be desired. Jerry was a sweetie, but ... I'd probably never really get to know him. I felt bad about that, guilty even, but it wasn't merely a matter of his stuttering. He got so nervous that it made me uncomfortable, and I couldn't see pursuing a relationship like that.

I lost Sean's footprints about halfway down the path. The ground got rockier there, so maybe I just wasn't seeing his tracks. I looked around the nearby storehouses to make sure nothing was damaged.

The slope had crumbled a little a few feet above the path. I noticed a small storehouse higher up on the cliff. It blended in with the rock so well that I wouldn't have noticed it if I hadn't been looking. It probably wasn't meant to be a hiding place, though; people had simply used the materials at hand.

The turned-up dirt on the slope looked fairly

fresh, but I couldn't tell if someone had stepped there or if the damage was entirely natural—maybe dislodged from a rock bouncing down from above. I glanced up toward the rim. I would have to be careful in case some passing tourist kicked a rock off the edge. I was about fifty feet down now, but if a rock bounced, it could reach me. I shuddered to think of it.

I turned and looked out over the canyon, a lovely expanse in shades of red and brown, with green down in the cool depths. It didn't seem like desert, despite the dryness. The word desert suggested emptiness, monotonous drifts of sand. Here the rich colors and rounded rock shapes drew you in. When you looked close, you saw a whole life of shrubs, cacti, mosses, and lichen, some of which the Ancestral Pueblo People used for food, medicine, or dye. They even used shredded bark for insulation and berries for jewelry, and, of course, wood for building or fires. It was hard to imagine surviving on natural resources here, but you could still glimpse the rich life they must have had.

Time to head back up for my gear. The dozen storehouses would keep me busy for a couple of weeks. Fortunately, the area had lots of little ledges, so I could set down my gear or find a rest spot when I needed it. I would enjoy working here, tucked away out of sight. People would be able to see me from the far canyon rim, but they wouldn't try to talk to me from there. I could stay in my own little world, coming out only when I felt up to facing company.

For the moment, I put living men—all of them—out of my mind. I had work to do. The secrets of the past seemed much more comfortable than the realities of the present.

Six

I spent several hours peering, probing, and scraping, in the process preparing two dozen slides that might or might not tell me anything. Finally I rose, stretched, and took the last long drink from my water bottle. Sweat dampened my skin and my stomach grumbled. Time for a break. I packed up my gear and climbed the path.

I headed for my campsite, wishing I had something more interesting than granola bars, nuts, and fruit for lunch. As I entered the campground, I saw the old woman at the host site, sitting at her picnic table—with Sean.

He got up and headed toward me, then glanced back to say, "Nice visiting with you, Mrs. West."

"You too, dear," her voice boomed out. She beamed at me as Sean joined me.

He gave me that appealing boyish grin. "You look hot and tired and thirsty. Seems like this is the perfect time to invite you to lunch again."

I looked at the old woman and back at Sean. Danesh had said Mrs. West learned everything about everybody. She and Sean had apparently had a long visit, and she seemed to approve of him. I had an unexpected second chance, but I wasn't sure what to do with it. Play it safe or take a risk?

"Indian tacos," Sean said temptingly. "Hot fry bread, meat, and green chile ... and a large soda with lots of ice ..."

My stomach rumbled so loud he must've heard, and I laughed. "All right, you've convinced me. Give me ten minutes to clean up."

Sean walked to my campsite with me and waited there while I washed up in the bathroom and changed my shirt. I stared at myself in the blurry metal mirror. Had I made the right choice? My stomach was knotting at the thought of getting in a car with a strange man. I tried to tell myself that the pain was only hunger. I couldn't live in fear forever.

I walked back to my campsite, determined to treat this "date" with the casual confidence it deserved.

Sean gestured at my tent. "Nice place you got."

I managed a smile, but it occurred to me that if I was anxious about getting in a car with a man I barely knew, I'd been stupid to let him see where I was staying, alone and without locks or even doors.

I tried to shake off the thoughts. I had to stop thinking that people were out to get me. The guy in Boston was scum with a previous record. And as for Jonathan—well, people let you down sometimes. Not everyone was ready to handle a crisis. But I had to believe that most people were decent. Constant paranoia was no way to live.

"Did you want to drive?" Sean frowned at my car. "That doesn't look built for the roads around here."

"It's not," I admitted.

"We can take my SUV. Up to you."

It made sense. It was a purely logical plan, and Sean wasn't pressuring me. But my hands were shaking as I got my bag. Get a grip, I told myself. You're just going out to lunch with a perfectly nice guy. I looked at him. "We can take your car. But I hope you won't think I'm completely nuts if I ask you to do something first."

He shrugged. "Anything."

"Show your ID to Mrs. West."

He frowned for a few seconds, but then his face cleared. "I get it. Prove I am who I say I am and leave a witness."

I glanced away. "You probably think it's stupid."

"No, it's smart. You're right to be cautious. Come on, I bet the old lady gets a kick out of it."

She did. And she waved us off like a gracious mother pleased about her daughter's first date. We walked back to the visitors center, where he'd parked his vehicle. I'd found a balance between being a coward and being rash, and Sean hadn't been offended at all.

We came out of the trees into the parking lot. Danesh was bent over a hoe in a little garden beside the building. I held my breath and resisted the urge to duck behind Sean. Danesh didn't glance our way, and I let out a sigh of relief once the building hid us from view. Not that it was any of his business where I went or with whom, but I doubted that would stop him from making comments.

Sean had a dark green SUV with leather seats and an impressive sound system. He either made a lot of money or was one of those guys who spent every penny on his car. It struck me that this was a Tuesday, and he apparently didn't have to work. "So what do you do? For a living, I mean."

He turned down the classic rock on the radio. "I was hoping you'd find the sense of mystery alluring. Better than the dull truth, anyway."

"Oh, come on," I said. "How bad can it be?"

He grinned. "Guess."

"Oh, all right. It's boring, you say? Um... accountant? Insurance agent?"

He shook his head.

"Hmm, you're off on a Tuesday... unless you work nights. Cleaning person? Street sweeper?"

That probably wouldn't buy him a vehicle like this. I had no idea, but he was smiling so I kept at it. "Wait, I got it—you're the guy who changes all the light bulbs in office buildings at night. Or you count ball bearings in the roller skate plant. You're a taste tester at the frozen fish stick factory."

He was laughing now. "You were closer in the beginning."

"You sell magazines by phone."

"I said I was dull, not desperate."

"Maybe you'd better just tell me."

"Maybe I should let you make something up," he said. "At least then I'd sound original."

I gave him a pleading look.

"Oh, all right. I'm a sales representative for a cell phone company."

"Well, that's...um, I mean...."

"It's OK, you don't have to say anything nice. I told you it sounds dull, especially to someone in your exciting field."

"Archeology only sounds exciting. It's mostly paperwork."

"My job involves a lot of paperwork, too. But I work independently, set my own hours, and the money's all right. I've paid off my student loan. I studied political science, but there aren't a lot of jobs in that field. I'd like to get involved with politics, but people won't take me seriously at my age. So for now I'm just making money. I may go back to college in a year or two, get an MBA."

"You don't have to defend your job. It sounds great." I adjusted the air vent and enjoyed the cool, not to mention the smooth ride over the washboard road. "I sure can't afford a car like this, with what I do. And none of us really knows what we'll be doing in five or ten years. There aren't many jobs in archeology. Maybe I'll be asking you for work."

He gave me a long look and a warm smile. "Any time." He asked about my research and sounded genuinely interested when I explained in detail. Then we talked about movies—the nearest theater was fifty miles away, but one of the trading posts showed movies once a week.

"If you get to explore Utah, stop in Moab," Sean said. "It's the shooting location for scenes from *Thelma and Louise* and the third Indiana Jones movie. A bunch of others, too. It even has the Hollywood Stuntmen's Hall of Fame."

I laughed. "What will my friends say if I go to the southwest desert and come back with stories of Hollywood?"

"Right, you're a big-city girl — you get real

entertainment, not the hick stuff we have out here in the boonies."

I hadn't meant to be insulting, but before I could explain, the song on the radio stopped, and a man's voice said, "And now for a special news update. We reported this morning that a small plane was seen flying low across the desert last night. Police say they've found no sign of a crash, as was feared."

Sean reached out as if to change the station, but I caught his arm. "Wait a minute, I saw a small plane yesterday, flying really low. Maybe someone reported it."

The announcer said, "Rumor has it that the plane may have been smuggling—"

"Which way was it headed?" Sean asked.

"Uh, east—no, northeast, I guess. The plane came toward the canyon and then turned and went alongside it."

"There's nothing much out that way. Probably a coincidence, and you saw a private pilot on a cross-country trip."

"I suppose." I tried to listen to the newscast while we talked but only caught a few words about investigations of a drug ring. It seemed strange that a drug ring would center here, practically in the middle of nowhere, but the announcer said something about an access point to Denver and Albuquerque. They were hours away, but obviously it wouldn't be as easy to land a plane secretly near a big city.

"Did you see the call letters on the plane?" Sean asked.

"The what?"

"Planes have to have identifying letters and numbers on the body."

I closed my eyes and tried to picture the plane. "I don't remember anything. It was probably too far to see it."

"Nothing much you can do about it, then, even if it was the same plane." Sean switched the radio off. "It's too good a day for bad news. Tell me about life in Boston. Do you have a ... significant other?"

I kept my eyes on the road. "No. Not anymore. I mean, not right now."

"Good." Sean settled back in his seat and smiled.

I smiled back. So what if my face felt a little stiff? I didn't have to do anything I didn't want to do. And I had plenty of time to decide on that.

A few minutes later, Sean said, "That's the town up ahead."

I could only see a few bumps on the horizon, but they did turn into a town, or at least a cluster of buildings. The diner sat on the main road with a big sign out front.

"The best place in town to eat," Sean said. "Okay, the only place. But it is good."

We went in and found a booth. The decor was nothing special—plastic checkered tablecloths, hard benches, and a few posters on the wall. "No menus," Sean said. "Just what they have on the board."

A chalkboard behind the counter listed red chile, green chile, and Indian tacos.

"Quite a selection," I said. "What's the difference between the red and green chile? And if you say color, I'll throw this hot sauce at you."

Sean grinned. "Green chiles turn red as they ripen. The green is usually hotter. Better stick with red if you're new to this; it's enough to burn the lining off your mouth. And chile really is just chile peppers, cooked with some onions and garlic, but no beans or meat unless you ask for it. The Indian tacos are fry bread with chile on top and beans or meat if you want. I recommend them."

A plump, middle-aged waitress came over. I ordered Indian tacos with red chile. Sean had the same. The food came out five minutes later, and I took a tentative bite.

I made a whimper of pain and breathed out around the scalding food in my mouth. When it finally cooled enough to chew, a different type of burning started.

I swallowed, took a deep drink, and then

demanded, "This is the less hot one? Are you playing a trick on me?"

"No, I swear!" Sean was laughing. "The green is even worse. But this is an especially hot year. Can you stand it?"

"I guess so. The flavor's good, at least what I can taste with my tongue throbbing."

"Better have a beer." Sean waved to the waitress. "That helps kill the burn."

I managed to eat the fry bread once I'd scraped half the chile off of it. After lunch we wandered the town and stopped at the general store. I grabbed the opportunity to get some ice for my cooler and a few perishable foods. When we got back in the car, I was surprised to see the clock on the dash reading three o'clock. Good thing I'd gotten a lot done that morning.

"You look serious," Sean said. "Anything wrong?"

"No. I was just deciding that I might as well blow off the rest of the day now."

"That's the spirit! Care for that hike?"

"Sure, why not? I haven't done the full trail yet. It's what, four or five miles?"

"I'll try to keep up," he said. "I don't suppose you could carry me back if I don't make it."

"I wouldn't try. But I might report it to the rangers. Eventually."

Sean laughed. "I'd better stick it out, then. Good thing I have a couple of water bottles in the car. I'll need to refill them, though."

"The campground has a pump." I wanted to avoid the visitors center. Danesh didn't need to know I was slacking off so much, especially after I refused to hike with him.

We stopped at the campground for water and then started the long walk around the canyon. Sean seemed to know everything about the region. He identified plants and birds, pointed out a snake basking in the sun, and told me about the nearby towns. I began to suspect that he knew plenty about the Ancestral Pueblo People, too. His morning request for a "guide" had obviously been a ruse, which made me smile. I wasn't used to men jumping so quickly on the chance to get to know me. They must be desperate for women around there.

We paused to catch our breath and take a drink. "You've been here your whole life?" I asked.

"Yep. Right here in this very spot." We looked around at the sagebrush and sand and laughed. "No, really, I was born in Blanding, but I went to college in Denver, and I've traveled a bit. Mexico, Guatemala, Belize—great scuba diving there. But this is home. I know it here, really know it, and there's something comforting about that."

I nodded. "It feels like you could know this land in a way you can't ever know a city like Boston, even if you know every street. Maybe because things change too fast in the city, but not here."

Sean chuckled. "No, here it takes decades just to get a road paved. But you're right, that's part of the charm."

We finished the loop near the ruin called Falling House, the one on an outcropping split off from the canyon rim by a five-foot gap. "Are you going to do any work here?" Sean asked.

"At this building?" I gazed at the walls across the gap. "No. It's great, I'd love to study it, but my work will be in the storehouses."

"They're easier to get to, anyway. Here you'd have to climb up the cliffs."

"Or build a bridge." I smiled at Sean. It was nice to spend time with a guy who was smart, easy-going, and funny. I was glad I'd taken the chance. Maybe I wasn't quite as scarred as I had feared. Maybe I was even ready to move forward. I wondered what the future would hold and felt a tingle of anticipation.

Seven

We neared the trail to the campground. Sean cleared his throat and gestured to a bench. "Care to sit for a minute?"

I nodded. We sat and gazed out over the canyon—the shadow-filled crevasse, the silhouettes of ruins scattered along the path, and the distant mesas turning rosy in the evening sun.

"Are you finding anything to do in the evenings?" Sean asked.

"I've only had one. But I'm looking forward to watching the sunsets and seeing the ruins by moonlight." I grinned. "Maybe keeping an eye out for ghosts or aliens."

Sean frowned. "Be careful at night. You should stay away from the canyon after dark."

Geez, they acted like the place really was full of ghosts or aliens or archaeologist-eating monsters.

Sean took my hand. I studied the scenery and focused on breathing.

"Kylie ..."

I turned and gazed into his intense green eyes. He brushed my cheek lightly with his free hand. Then he leaned in and kissed me.

Maybe he sensed my tension; he started slow. I tried to stop thinking and enjoy the sensation of warm lips on mine. He stroked a hand up my back and feathered kisses over my cheek and neck. I felt myself relax, like slipping into a warm bath, and when his mouth came back to mine, I met him eagerly. The kiss set off a kind of trembling I hadn't felt in months—a good kind.

When he eased back I let out a long sigh. I could enjoy this again. That was good to know.

Sean said, "I wish I didn't have to go."

"You need to leave?" Disappointment warred with relief.

"I'm afraid so. I have to be somewhere tonight and I'm already running late. You're too tempting." He gave me another gentle kiss. "I'll see you soon?"

"I hope so."

"I can't tomorrow. Maybe Thursday. You have a phone?"

"Yes, but it doesn't get reception very well out here, and I'm keeping it off so I don't have to worry about charging so often." I thought of the visitors center, but I didn't want romantic messages left there. "You can text me, though. I'll try to check messages a couple of times a day."

"Tell you what," he said. "You get some work done tomorrow. We'll go out Thursday, about five. I'll buy you a good meal and we can see a movie. And ... maybe I shouldn't suggest this. I don't want you to take it wrong, but if you're ready for a hot shower, we can stop by my apartment first thing." He grinned. "Purely a selfless and generous offer, I promise."

"You mean you want a clean date. That is tempting." I decided not to commit to the shower until I'd had time to consider. "Okay, we'll call it a provisional plan. Text me if anything changes."

He programmed my number into his phone. "Shall I escort you back to the campground?"

"No, I'll sit here a few more minutes. But thanks."

"You're not going to do any work tonight, I hope?"

"No. I just don't feel like heading back yet." And I didn't want a romantic goodbye in front of the camp host, a known gossip.

He stood and laid a hand on my shoulder. "Okay, but stay out of the canyon at night. You could stumble on a snake or scorpion, slip on a rock and break your ankle ..."

I sighed. "I know. I'll be careful."

"I know you're capable of taking care of yourself. But the dangers here are different from in the city, and I wouldn't want anything to happen to you."

I smiled up at him. "I'll stay here five minutes and then go back to my campsite. Lunch is wearing off anyway."

He cupped my cheek in his hand. "All right. I'll see you soon."

After he left, I stared at the scenery and tried to make sense of my feelings. I wouldn't fool myself into thinking this was some big love affair, but I'd had a good time, and I hadn't humiliated myself by having hysterics when he kissed me. I was proving something to myself.

I frowned. Was I using Sean? What if he took this more seriously than I did?

I shrugged. You couldn't plan a relationship from the first date. Maybe my feelings would change. Maybe he didn't expect anything more than a few casual dates. Of course, men almost always did expect—or at least want—sex even if their emotions were casual. I couldn't even blame them, since it was a biological urge. Well, if Sean wanted sex right away, I'd tell him what had happened to me. He'd either slow down or disappear entirely. Problem solved.

I closed my eyes and tipped my head back. A bird chirped and rustled in the trees and then went silent. The air lay warm and heavy. The whole canyon seemed still, waiting.

It should have been relaxing, but I felt a prickle on the back of my neck. I shivered and opened my eyes, glancing around quickly. No one in sight. So why did I have the sudden feeling I was being watched?

Nerves. I sighed. I still couldn't tell the difference between solid warning instincts and unreasonable panic. Regardless, the peaceful mood had been broken. I jumped when something shook the bushes nearby. Time to head back to my campsite, where I had privacy within shouting distance of people.

I was halfway to the campground when I heard a low rumble. I paused, senses on alert. Then I blew out a breath and relaxed. Since when did I jump at a car engine starting—a sound I wouldn't even notice in the city? The sound softened to a steady hum and faded as the car moved away. I realized I hadn't heard Sean's vehicle earlier, so that was probably him. He must have stopped at the campground restroom or something.

As I turned down the path to the campground, my stomach grumbled, and I debated the ease of granola bars and fruit versus the satisfaction of a hot meal. I decided I might as well set up my camp stove. I'd be camping for weeks, and woman could not survive on snack food alone, so I might as well start a good habit.

The smell of grilled meat drifted past me. I inhaled deeply and my stomach growled louder. I spotted the old couple at the host site. The man stood over a raised metal grill as the woman came out of the camper with a pack of buns and an armload of condiments. She waved the hand with the buns and called out. "You made it back!"

"I sure did." I had to smile. She talked like I'd been on a dangerous cross-country trek.

She dropped her food on the table and came toward me, holding out her hand. "We didn't meet properly before. Lily West." The name Lily didn't fit her low, gravelly voice, mannish haircut, and square jaw. I wondered whether she had been slim and graceful in her youth. "That's my husband, Robert," she added. He raised his tongs in salute.

"Kylie Hafford."

She beamed. "The archaeologist. I wasn't expecting such a cute young thing."

She obviously meant well, so I smiled and said, "I'm older than I look."

"Stay to dinner." She took my arm to lead me to the table, as if the matter were settled. When I hesitated, she said, "We always have plenty."

I glanced at the grill and gaped at the huge

number of hot dogs, probably two dozen. I never ate hot dogs at home, but they smelled heavenly and my stomach demanded food. "All right. Thank you."

I tried to think of something else to say, but Lily didn't need much help. "We like this job because we get to meet people. We travel around the country, staying for a month or a few at different sites. It's a great way to see places and meet new people. And it's cheap! Some of the popular sites are booked up years in advance, but we like the small ones anyway, don't we, Robert?"

He didn't bother to answer, and she didn't wait. "We've been here six weeks. It's getting a little warm now, but—" She broke off and waved. "Come on in! Don't be afraid, this is our new friend, Kylie."

More company? I turned to see two children, maybe ages three and six, hovering at the edge of the trees. I thought they were both boys, though with their shaggy hair and dirty faces it was hard to tell. Lily pulled out hot dog buns and squirted them with ketchup and mustard, then jumped up and hurried to the grill. Robert placed hot dogs in the buns without glancing in the direction of the children.

Lily carried the hot dogs to the kids, who hadn't moved. "You want to take some to your folks?" she asked. The older boy shook his head, his suspicious gaze still on me. He took the hot dogs and led his little brother back into the trees. They hadn't said a word.

Lily sat down with a sigh. "Poor little mites. At least we know they're getting fed."

"Who are they?"

"Their parents have the last campsite back in that corner. Out of work—I got that much from the mother, though she's a mousy little thing and almost as quiet as her boys. They haven't paid their campground fee in a couple of weeks, but we haven't had the heart to say anything."

"But why are they here?"

Lily shrugged. "Too proud to go to a shelter, I suppose. It's quiet here this time of year."

I guessed that was the man I'd seen the morning before, but Lily changed the subject, talking about the other people in the campground. Some she barely knew, if they'd just arrived, though it sounded like she did her best to get a full family history of everyone.

I had assumed the campground would be impersonal, a group of strangers only loosely tied by proximity, like an apartment building where you nodded to your neighbors in passing but didn't know their names. Instead I'd stumbled into an odd little community.

Of course, it didn't take long for Lily's curiosity to turn on me.

I answered her questions about school and my research without hesitation. She surprised me into admitting that I had been engaged, but that it'd ended six months ago.

"So you don't have a young man waiting for you back in Boston?" she asked.

"No, no one is waiting for me. Anywhere."

Lily gave me a significant look. "So you're free, if a nice young man should happen to come along out here."

I was trying to think how to answer when her husband spoke for almost the first time. "Don't mind her. She likes to meddle. It's, what do you call it, living vicariously."

Lily burst into low guffaws worthy of Santa Claus.

I smiled and decided that was a good time to take my leave. "I don't mind. But I'd better head back to my own campsite. Thanks for dinner." I slid off the bench.

"Oh, don't run away," Lily said. "You must get bored and lonely over there by yourself, and you can't tell me it's bedtime yet."

It didn't feel like bedtime, and I already knew how challenging it was trying to read in the light of a small battery-powered lantern while lying in my sleeping bag. But I'd had all the company I could take for one day. "I'm going to go to the visitors center and do some work. I got a late start today. But thanks again!"

Once I'd had the idea, I liked it. I could fill my evening and make up for slacking off earlier. I'd have light and a comfortable chair. I could take a look at the slides I'd prepared at the storehouses and see whether I was getting anything of interest. That would help me target the next day's work.

Darkness had fallen by the time I gathered my microscope and slides plus the paperwork I needed to finish. I held the box of equipment awkwardly in one arm so I could carry a flashlight in my other hand and took the path through the woods. When I got to the parking lot, I glanced up. Stars seemed to be blinking on, more every few seconds. I turned off my flashlight and watched until a kind of vertigo made me sway. Our planet really was only a speck in the universe. But what a universe it was!

The night breeze caressed my face. The wind shook the trees, making the forest sound alive. But the sound didn't frighten me the way a single rustling in a bush did. The trees were not my enemies. An owl hooted, a lonely sound that sent a thrill rippling up my spine. I could almost hear the canyon calling me, whispering of mystery and romance. This wasn't an opportunity to pass up.

I left the box by the door and walked to the canyon, entranced by the night. I wouldn't be foolish enough to go exploring, but I wanted to stand on the rim and let the atmosphere soak in. I paused several feet back from the rim and let the night air wash over me as I listened to the breeze whispering in the trees.

Or was it the breeze? It sounded like human voices, faint and ghostly. But I didn't believe in ghosts. It had to be something else.

I studied the darkness, straining my ears to locate the sound. A light flicked on a hundred yards away. It moved briefly and I could see the outline of a crumbled wall. Somebody was in one of the ruins.

I took a few steps forward and then stopped. I should do something, but what? If I really was hearing voices, that suggested at least two people. It was probably some kids exploring or one of those crystal worshipers Danesh had mentioned. But what if it wasn't someone so harmless? I couldn't imagine what thieves would be doing here, where everything valuable and portable had already been removed, but I knew some sites attracted bandits and they could be armed and dangerous.

I didn't want to confront strangers alone. Danesh and Jerry were long gone and miles away. The old couple at the host site was supposed to keep an eye on things at night, but I didn't want to drag them into something potentially dangerous. I didn't know anyone else in the campground.

I could get closer and start waving my light around and calling out to try to scare them, but that might backfire. If they were kids, they might try to escape down the canyon, where they could get hurt. I could wait and try to get a look at them when they left, but the wind was already raising goosebumps on my skin, and I'd foolishly neglected to bring a sweater. I'd be fine when moving, but standing around in the cold night air did not appeal. And if I went back to my campsite for another layer, chances were they'd have moved on before I returned.

I watched for another minute and then reluctantly decided it might be better to do nothing. A confrontation could lead to injury, and I didn't have the authority to do more than scold them anyway. I sighed and turned back toward the visitors center.

I let myself in and flicked on the lights, then carried my box of equipment to the counter. The two small windows here were black squares. No need for heavy curtains to keep out the glare of streetlights. But if someone looked in, they'd be able to see me and I probably wouldn't be able to see them. A gust of wind rattled the windows. The floor creaked when I shifted my weight. And yet the building seemed too quiet. I was still more at home with the rumble of traffic and voices outside my window.

"There's no need to get jumpy." My voice sounded strange, but I kept speaking aloud. "Your anxiety is a reaction to triggers. It's all right to be afraid, but that doesn't mean you are really in danger." The now-familiar calming technique helped settle me. I couldn't always control my emotions or my body's sensations, but I could control my behavior. The old "mind over matter" worked—sometimes—once you'd had training.

I could more easily convince myself I was safe if I made sure I was protected, so I crossed the room and locked the front door. Then I went into the back room and fixed a cup of tea, trying to clear my mind by focusing closely on that mundane task. Finally I settled down to work.

As always, the work helped. I quickly got so caught up that I forgot everything except what I saw through the microscope.

Something jolted me back to awareness. I lifted my head and listened. What had I heard?

Probably nothing. Normal night sounds. They just weren't normal to me.

Or maybe whoever had been in the ruin was leaving. A glance at the clock showed me that over an hour had passed, which seemed a long time for anyone to be poking around in ruins, but if it was them, maybe I could get a look. I went to one of the small windows and looked out, but with the glare from the inside light and the darkness outside, I couldn't see much. I crossed to the door and hesitated. Should I stick my head out and check? Or stay safely inside?

My hand hovered over the door handle. I couldn't hide away forever. Sometimes you have to face your fears.

Pounding rattled the door. I jumped back with a gasp.

A voice outside yelled, "Help! Let us in!"

Eight

"Kylie! Open up!" The voice was low and rough, that of a man—or Lily West.

I fumbled for the door handle and pulled open the door. Lily pushed past me, dragging someone behind her. "Close the door," she said between gasping breaths.

I closed and locked it, then turned to stare at the little group huddled in the center of the room—Lily, holding the younger boy from dinner, and a thin woman clutching the hand of the older child. The children stared with enormous eyes but didn't move or make a sound. Soft sobbing came from the woman.

"The phone," Lily said. "Call 911."

I crossed to the counter. "What's happened? Is someone hurt?"

"Not yet," Lily said. "We need the police."

My hand shook as I dialed, and I clutched the receiver so hard my fingers hurt. I heard myself give my name and our location as if listening to someone else from a distance.

Someone pounded on the door. We all jumped, and the woman screamed.

Outside, a man yelled and swore, demanding to be let in.

"Robert was trying to slow him down," Lily said. "Oh, Robert—" She looked gray, and I hoped she wasn't going to faint with the child still in her arms.

"You'd better send an ambulance, too," I said into the phone. "Yes, I'll stay on the line." I put my hand over the receiver. "Lily. Lily!"

She slowly turned her head to look at me.

"Take them into the back room. Make some tea. There might be cocoa for the children."

She took a deep breath and gave a little shake, then nodded briskly and headed for the back room. "Come on." The other woman trailed after her, dragging the older boy. He glared at me as he passed, as if this were somehow my fault, or maybe he simply didn't like a stranger seeing his family's problems.

The pounding on the door stopped. I waited, darting glances between the windows. Would he try them next?

Something slammed against the door with an astounding crash. I gasped and dropped the phone. He must have either thrown himself against the door or tried to kick it down. It held, but for how long?

I looked around for anything to brace the door. I grabbed a rack of brochures and wedged it under the door handle, but I didn't think the flimsy wire would do much good. I needed a weapon. I ran back to the counter and searched the shelves underneath. Brochures, papers, office supplies, T-shirts. I got down on hands and knees and ducked my head under the bottom shelf to check the back corners. Nothing more dangerous than a heavy book or a ballpoint pen.

The man crashed against the door again. I jerked back, cracking my head on the underside of the counter.

I rubbed my head as I stood and darted to the back room. The thin woman and the children were huddled on the couch. Lily stood solidly in the middle of the room, holding a toilet plunger like a baseball bat. I let out a half hysterical gasp.

"It's the best thing I could find," Lily said.

Another crash was followed by the tinkle of shattered glass hitting the floor. I whipped around and looked into the front room. A face loomed at one of the windows and I shied back. "How big is this guy?" I asked.

Lily stepped up beside me. "He's too big to get

through one of those windows."

I nodded but closed the door between the rooms, just in case.

"You got the police?" Lily asked.

"Yes. Wait, the phone." It still lay on the counter, and I didn't want to go back to the other room. "It doesn't matter. They know we're here and we're in trouble. And they're probably listening to that." I bobbed my head toward the door and the sounds of the man's curses.

"It'll take time," Lily murmured, too soft for the others to hear.

I nodded. Unless a police car happened to be already on the road out here, we wouldn't get help for twenty or thirty minutes. I took a deep breath. "Then I guess we'd better be ready."

We shoved a file cabinet in front of the door. Fortunately, this back room had no windows.

The water Lily had put in the microwave was hot, so I made tea for the adults and cocoa for the children. I hoped that this simple task would help me stay steady and a warm drink might comfort them.

Plus, hot liquid and a heavy mug made tolerable weapons.

I seemed to be watching myself from a distance, mildly surprised that I was acting calmly and sensibly—that I was acting at all. Had I really improved so much in the last six months? Or was it because this wasn't directly my problem? Because it was easier to help someone else than myself?

When I handed the woman a mug of tea, she was shaking so badly she splashed some in her lap. She kept her gaze down, avoiding my eyes. I cupped my hand under hers and gently lifted the mug toward her mouth. "Drink."

I wanted to say, "It will be all right," but I couldn't force the lie. We might get through this night, but she had a long road ahead. Would she be strong enough to handle it?

I smiled at the boys, but they looked so wary I

didn't dare touch them. I wished I had a couple of stuffed animals to offer.

"Listen," Lily said.

I had half-turned and was reaching toward my mug still on the counter. We froze like a tableau, the woman's mug halfway to her parted lips, Lily's head cocked to one side.

I could still hear shouting, but something had changed. More than one voice rose outside. After a couple of minutes, they faded. A knock came at the door, a sharp *rat-a-tat-tat* but without the earlier violence. Then a voice—"Lily! Lily, you all right?"

She put her hand to her chest. "Robert."

"Surely it's too soon for the police," I said.

She frowned and shook her head. Robert kept calling.

"He'll be worried," Lily said. We shoved the file cabinet away from the door.

"Wait here," I told the mother and children as Lily opened the door.

Robert was peering through the broken window. He gave a glad cry at the sight of Lily. She rushed to the front door and moments later they were embracing.

I held onto the front door, ready to slam it shut, as I looked outside. A half-dozen people milled around. I vaguely recognized a woman I'd seen in the bathroom and a couple who had been sitting at a picnic table when I passed by earlier.

The gay couple stood close together, watching a man seated on the ground with his head down. Blood dripped from one fist; he must have punched through the window. A young man stood over him as if ready to pounce should he get out of line.

The gay man formerly in blue glanced up and waved. He crossed to me and asked, "Is everyone all right?"

I nodded. "Where—why—"

"We heard the commotion at the campground. We weren't sure what was happening, but then—"

He gestured at Robert. "He said women and

children were in trouble and needed help."

Well. "Thanks."

He shrugged. "We didn't do much. Just showed up. He backed down pretty quickly when he saw all of us."

I smiled. "Sometimes showing up is enough."

Robert came up and patted my shoulder. I glanced back to see that Lily had gone into the other room. I wondered if I should join her, but she already had a rapport with the family. Another face might make them more anxious.

The police showed up ten or fifteen minutes later. They put the violent man in the back of the police car and started taking statements. Lily said she and Robert would look after the woman and children until everything got sorted out. "Maybe now she'll take my hints about a shelter," she whispered to me.

I smiled and blinked back tears. "Thank you."

Her eyes widened. "For what? Dragging you into this trouble?"

"For being the kind of person who helps." I hugged her.

The thin woman tried to scurry by with her head down, but I reached out to stop her. When she flinched, I dropped my hand, but I had to speak. "Keep asking for help. You deserve it." She didn't look up, but after a moment she gave a tiny nod.

I wished I could do more for her, but at least I had done something. I had been there when needed, which not everyone could claim. And as I had learned in my own quest to embrace life again, the first step really was just showing up.

Nine

An odd atmosphere had fallen over the group, half party, half funeral, with whispers and nervous laughter. People were excited to be part of the solution, even as they mourned the problem.

I still felt somewhat outside of myself, like a distant observer even though I'd been in the middle of things. I went around the side of the building, a little separate from the rest of the crowd. A chicken-wire fence outlined the small garden plot where I'd seen Danesh working earlier. Several of the metal posts holding up the fence were topped by fist-sized squash, making a funky accent and showing off the ancient vegetable.

I ran a hand over one of the squash, feeling slight bumps and ridges in the smooth skin, and then looked down into the garden. The moon had risen and cast light on the bushy plants and trailing vines. Even here, in the high desert, if you tended things properly, they grew. Such a simple thing, a garden. Simple things get you grounded when the world seems crazy.

I reached over the waist-high fence and rubbed a velvety leaf between my fingers. "This is reality too," I whispered. I focused on the air temperature, comfortably cool, the feel of the ground beneath my feet, the murmur of voices behind me, and the distant hooting of an owl. I started to feel part of the world again.

The police car drove away. People headed back to the campground. I swayed with exhaustion, but I remembered the broken glass. I needed to clean up, turn off the lights, lock the door. And in the morning I would have to explain the broken window.

I walked through the door and stared at Danesh, who was sweeping glass into a dustpan. "When did you get here?" I asked.

"A few minutes ago. I heard the news report that police had been called out."

"It was on the news? But it just happened!"

He gave his patented half-smile. "The DJ at the local radio station keeps his police scanner on."

I hesitated, then closed the front door behind me and came further into the room. "You know what happened?"

He gave a single nod, frowning, and carried the broken glass to the garbage. "Are you all right?"

"I'm fine. We just had a few bad minutes. You know, you really need some kind of weapon in here."

"Yeah." He pushed a hand through his hair. "Never thought about it before. We keep the good weapons in the shed."

"Excuse me?"

His smile flashed on and disappeared. "Hoes, shovels, things like that. Those are probably the best weapons around, but they're locked up in the little shed behind the building."

"Oh." I crossed to the counter and started putting away my equipment. I felt the need to fill the silence. "I guess this explains some of the stuff that's been happening. Thefts of food and equipment—he was out of work and broke, according to Lily. Took it out on his wife, I guess."

I remembered the lights and voices. Was he to blame for that, too? What would a man like that be doing in the canyon? Hoping to find some overlooked treasure he could sell?

And what about the two voices I thought I'd heard? Could on out-of-work abuser really be responsible for all the strange activity here?

Danesh came over to stand beside me. "I'm sorry you had to go through that."

"Yeah. Me, too." I paused. "Though not really. I'm

glad I was here to help. I'm glad I could." I suddenly found myself shaking. Why now? I pressed my hands down on the counter and tried to lock my knees so I wouldn't fall.

Danesh put a hand on my shoulder. I flinched, but he kept the connection. I could feel the warmth through my shirt despite his light touch.

He slowly turned me toward him. He slid his arms around me.

I pressed my cheek against his shoulder. My breathing came in harsh gasps. I wrapped my arms around Danesh's waist and he tightened his grip.

"It's all right," he whispered. "It's over now."

It should have been over, at least for me. But memories flashed through my mind, from another day, yet as strong as if they were happening now. I squeezed my eyes closed but I didn't try to banish the visions. I let them play out—

A dark shape leaping out at me as I jogged past a cluster of bushes. The shock, the utter astonishment, that caused me to fall limp as the man dragged me into those bushes. The feel of hands groping me through my thin T-shirt and shorts and then underneath them.

The swirling panic and helplessness.

Vomit rising in my throat as screams echoed in my mind but wouldn't come out. The humiliation of lying in a heap, sobbing, as a dog barked and my attacker ran away.

I clung to Danesh and remembered it all.

But I hadn't been so helpless this time. I had reached out to someone else in trouble. I hadn't let fear or panic keep me from acting. I could learn from the past and face the future. I had to, if I wanted a life worth living.

Finally my breathing slowed and my trembling stopped. I pushed back from Danesh and wiped at my eyes. "Thanks."

"Any time."

I grimaced and looked away from his steady gaze. "I hope there won't be a lot of times I need that."

"We all need it sometimes."

I made a noncommittal sound and moved away to gather up the rest of my equipment. It was hard to believe a man like Danesh ever needed a hug. But it was nice of him to try to make me feel less awkward. Unless he was simply warning me that the hug didn't mean anything. He didn't have to worry—I could tell the difference between passion and comfort.

I felt my cheeks heating under his gaze. I grabbed my box and turned, but he was blocking the end of the counter. I managed a smile. "I guess the excitement is over for the night, so I'll get going."

He took the box from me. "I'll walk you to your tent."

I opened my mouth to protest, but the truth was I would feel better with an escort. Being independent didn't mean I had to do everything alone. I stepped out into the parking lot and looked up at the sky as Danesh struggled to lock the damaged door. I thought about his hug, the surprising gentleness and understanding, when so many men got awkward or annoyed around tears. I was seeing a new side of him. Why was that so surprising, when I barely knew him?

Maybe my instinctive negative reaction to Danesh was only a result of discomfort left over from our first encounter. When I thought back, I couldn't remember a single thing he'd done that was really wrong. Irritating, maybe, but not cruel or unfair. Even his bossiness was of an overprotective nature, and there were a lot of worse qualities a man could have than protectiveness.

We'd shared a close moment. I could step away and reassert the distance or take this chance to get to know someone who might prove interesting.

I looked around the parking lot, now empty except for Danesh's truck, but somehow holding the echoes of the night's events. I didn't want the bad memories to take over this place and keep me from enjoying my time here. This was my place, for now, with everything it held—including Danesh.

I smiled as he joined me. "What's with the garden, anyway?" I asked, gesturing toward it.

"It's mainly a demonstration garden, though we do eat the produce. Squash and beans, like the Ancient Ones. A complete protein—but I'm sure you know that."

"Seeing as how my specialty is ancient foods," I agreed.

"Maybe you'll find evidence of something else they ate, and we'll have to update our garden."

"Maybe. That would be nice."

He tapped one of the squash stuck on top of a fence post. "Nothing is ready to harvest yet, but we keep these old, dried squash so people can see how they differ from the modern version. If you're here when this year's crop ripens, I'll cook some for you."

"Thanks." I couldn't think of anything else to say as we walked down the path. We had shared a moment of closeness, but I still felt awkward. My first impressions might have been wrong, but they had let me keep my distance. It wasn't easy to get involved in other people's lives.

I thought of Sean, Lily and Robert West, the crying woman and her solemn children. I couldn't get much more involved.

We reached my campsite and I opened the car trunk so he could deposit the box. "Well, thanks," I said, not looking at Danesh.

He didn't answer. I thought I could feel him staring at me again, but when I glanced over I saw him scanning the perimeter with narrowed eyes, like a soldier checking for the enemy. I was pretty sure the only danger was now in custody, but I watched him with a smile. It was rather nice to have someone looking out for me for a change.

He met my gaze. "You're sure you don't mind being alone here tonight?"

And what if I said I did? Would he offer to stay? I almost laughed. "I'm fine now. Thanks."

He nodded. "Sleep well." A moment later he had vanished among the trees.

I suddenly felt so exhausted I couldn't even bear the thought of walking to the restrooms to brush my teeth. I kicked off my boots and crawled into my sleeping bag.

Right before I drifted off to sleep, I realized I had forgotten to tell Danesh about the voices and lights in the ruins.

Ten

Despite the night's adventures—or maybe even because of them—I slept well and woke refreshed. I got to work and finished taking samples from two more storehouses. When I found a pale residue I didn't think was sand, I fixed and labeled two slides and tucked them into my sample box. I found some seeds as well, but they were probably recent additions, deposited by a rodent.

I was on my elbows and knees halfway in the storehouse with my rear sticking out when I heard a hello. I wriggled backward and turned to see Danesh walking down the path. I shaded my eyes and smiled up at him. "Thanks for not sneaking up on me—this time."

He grinned. "I'm learning. Though you are awfully cute when you're mad. How about some lunch? We picked up sandwiches."

He brushed right past the "cute" comment, so I decided I could ignore it. "Sounds good."

I followed Danesh up the path, admiring his smooth, light-footed stride, which hardly disturbed a pebble. I never would have heard him if he hadn't called out. I guess he really had made a special effort not to startle me.

As I thought of that first encounter, I found myself wishing he were wearing shorts and no shirt again. I remembered the feel of his arms around me the night before, warm and very male, yet gentle and comforting. When he reached the rim and waited for me, my smile felt stiff and I couldn't meet his gaze. Apparently my libido had started up again and was showing an alarming lack of discrimination. I kept my mouth shut and my eyes straight ahead during the rest of the walk.

Jerry smiled as I entered the visitors center and waved me to the back room. I sank onto the sofa, grateful to escape the sun for a while. Jerry pointed to three paper-wrapped sandwiches on the table. "I g-got ham, turkey, and veg-vegetarian. You choose."

"I'll take turkey, if that's all right."

"It's fine," Danesh said, picking up the vegetarian. "Jerry will eat anything."

I wondered if he was teasing Jerry about his weight. But Jerry was smiling and nodding as he picked up the ham sandwich. I had to stop jumping to conclusions and assuming the worst. I'd decided to be friendly, so it was time to tone down my overactive defenses.

I unwrapped the sandwich and bit through thick layers of meat and cheese between fragrant sourdough bread. People certainly knew how to eat in this little corner of nowhere. Danesh passed around sodas from the little fridge, and the cold cola tasted like heaven after a morning of hard work with only a bottle of increasingly hot water to ease my thirst.

As I listened to the men talk, I wondered how Jerry felt when Danesh finished his sentences for him. I'd felt the temptation myself sometimes but had resisted. Did Jerry feel hurt or angry when people literally took the words right out of his mouth? Or was he relieved to be understood quickly, so he didn't have to struggle through the rest of his statement?

It was a sad side effect of our polite society that you couldn't simply ask outright how someone felt or what he wanted. You had to guess and hope for the best. Or the worst, depending on your attitude.

I regretted that I would probably never get to know Jerry well and wondered how many others found it easier to avoid his friendship rather than work for it.

Danesh turned to me. "You told us about school. What do you do for fun? Or don't you have time for that?"

"School is fun. But I do other things. I'm on an intramural softball team. I like to go dancing or hang out at a bar."

Maybe I shouldn't have included that last statement. They might be picturing crummy dives with alcoholic bums, not the casual, student-friendly bars around Harvard Square.

"I don't suppose you do much hiking," Danesh said.

"Not by your definition. I go city hiking. Boston is a great city for walking. You can take the subway somewhere and then wander for hours. There are some great historical walking tours."

Danesh glanced at my legs. "Keeps you in shape, anyway. Hiking is my favorite pastime. Not much else to do around here. Outside, anyway."

I wondered what he was implying about indoor activities. He took another bite of his sandwich, with no sly smile to show he was suggesting something, but he wasn't the easiest guy to read. I, on the other hand, was probably turning pink as visions of Danesh getting indoor "exercise" filled my mind.

"What po-po-position?" Jerry asked.

"What?" For a moment I thought Jerry had read my mind. Then I realized what he meant. "Oh, shortstop mostly. We trade around, though."

"Wo-would you l-l-like—" he seemed to get totally stuck and turned Danesh with a pleading gesture.

"Hey, that's right! Maureen's team is playing today, right?"

When Jerry nodded, Danesh explained. "Maureen is Jerry's girlfriend. She plays on a city league—strictly fun, you know. More about drinking beer and trading jokes than winning. I'm sure they'd be happy to have a visiting player."

"That ... sounds like fun." Playing softball with a bunch of strangers wasn't on top of my to-do list, but I was still processing the information that Jerry had a girlfriend and feeling guilty that I was so surprised.

Danesh glanced at the clock on the wall. "What time's the game?"

"Six," Jerry said.

"So if we leave here right at five, we'll make it. They usually have a pizza break, and afterward everyone goes out for drinks."

Apparently it was settled. I was starting to like the idea, though. I told myself it would be rude to turn down Jerry's kind offer, but in reality I couldn't wait to get a look at the girlfriend. Plus, pizza! If I kept up this hectic social life, I'd never have to cook for myself. "I'll be here at five."

"Bring that shirt. I'll take it home and wash it."

I glanced down at my uniform shirt and wrinkled my nose. "Thanks for the hint. You're the one who told me to wear it every day." I stood and tossed my sandwich wrapper into the garbage. "I guess if you're going to wash it, there's no point in holding back now. A few more hours of work and it should be totally funky. I hope you don't pass out in your car from the fumes."

Danesh grinned up at me. "We'll toss it in the trunk. Don't work too hard. And I mean that. The heat is ferocious this time of day."

"I'll be careful." How many times did I have to repeat that statement? But he meant well. We'd all enjoy this month more if I let those comments go. But I would be careful not to get heat stroke, if only because I didn't want to prove him right.

I worked for another two hours before I had to concede defeat. I felt limp from the heat and my head pounded from the sun, so I decided to take a break in the cool bottom of the canyon.

I found a nice boulder at the edge of the river, took off my boots and socks, and soaked my feet until they felt numb and I started to shiver in the spray of cool water.

I backed away from the river and had a snack while my feet dried. It was almost four o'clock, so I had a little time before I had to change clothes and meet the guys. I couldn't do much of a tour, but I could visit one or two structures and use my official shirt as an excuse to take a closer look. I remembered the lights from the night before and tried to decide where they might have been. The best bet seemed like the ruin known as Eroded Boulder House. I took the path up to the canyon rim and headed for that site.

The Ancestral Pueblo People had taken advantage of a natural formation—an enormous rock with one side eroded underneath, forming an overhang something like a porch roof. The ancient builders had used the boulder for the roof and back wall, building three more walls to enclose the unit. Most of the stones had fallen from the outer walls, leaving rubble scattered around the boulder, but some interior walls still stood.

This ruin was one of the most accessible from the trail, and visitors were actually allowed to go inside. I skirted the boulder until I could enter the ruin. I had to crouch to get through the low doorway, even with part of the wall collapsed. Once inside, I stayed in a crouch. The Ancestral Pueblo People had been even shorter than I was.

I paused to let my eyes adjust before glancing around. After the bright light outside, I couldn't see much detail. As I turned to go, a glint of white against the reddish-brown stones caught my attention. A crumpled piece of paper. Why couldn't people be more careful with their litter?

I grabbed the paper and went back outside. The paper contained a crude drawing—a sort of puffy Y-shape with marks on it. Random doodles? Secret code?

The drawing seemed vaguely familiar. I turned it sideways, then upside down. Where had I seen that shape before?

I almost laughed. The canyon! Like the diagram in my guidebook, the Y-shape showed only this end, where the ruins were clustered. The marks must indicate some of the ruins, though it didn't have all of them. Some were marked with little squares, and one with an X. X marks the spot? Buried treasure?

Could it have anything to do with the lights and voices the previous night? I shook my head. Most likely some kids' game. The only children I'd seen were the poor little boys from last night. Surely they were too young to be running around on their own after dark. Though, on reflection, I had to admit that it was probably no more dangerous than staying with their parents. I didn't have much experience with kids, but those two certainly were frighteningly self-possessed and had been on their own when I first met them. I wondered if they were still with the Wests or if they had been taken to town.

I crumpled the paper to throw it away but hesitated. Should I show it to Danesh and Jerry? They might want to know if someone was playing games in their ruins. But the whole thing seemed harmless. I didn't see any damage or anything out of place. And I certainly didn't want anyone questioning those two little boys. They might already be gone and never come back, but if they did, I didn't want anyone harassing them. The Wests would keep an eye on them.

I would forget about what I had seen. We'd had enough trouble last night. I didn't need to start more. I had enough to worry about with a night of "local color" ahead.

Eleven

I checked my watch. Time to be getting to the visitors center. I was looking forward to the evening but also nervous about meeting a big group of new people. What if I didn't like anybody? What if they didn't like me? Playing softball should be okay, because we had something to do. I could plead exhaustion and skip out on the bar afterward if I didn't feel comfortable. At least I was getting involved. I was showing up, even if I wasn't comfortable yet.

I wondered if I'd run into Sean. This area couldn't have too many options for social interaction. And coincidences happened just when you thought they couldn't. Not that I really cared, but it would be funny if he turned out to be on the softball team or something.

I went back to the campground and washed up, but I knew nothing would make much of a difference if I were going to spend an hour in a hot car and then play softball. I'd bring my brush and mascara so I could primp a bit afterward, but this didn't seem like the region for big makeup jobs.

Finally I hopped in my car and drove the half-mile to the visitors center. I arrived at ten minutes to five and saw a car and a truck in the parking lot. I assumed they belonged to Jerry and Danesh, but when I went inside I saw a young couple standing at the counter. Jerry handed a camping permit to the man.

The woman, not much more than twenty with wavy, bottle-blonde hair, leaned across the counter toward Danesh. "Do you lead any walks or fireside chats?" she asked, with emphasis on the "you."

"Sometimes. There's a nature walk every morning at ten, and Sunday night a storyteller will present some folktales. He's really good."

"I'm so interested in learning about your people," she purred.

Danesh met my eyes over the woman's head and said without expression, "If you want to learn about the Pueblo Indians, you should visit one of the Pueblos or the Indian Pueblo Cultural Center in Albuquerque."

She started to speak but her boyfriend or husband put his arm around her and growled, "Come on, let's go."

As he dragged her away, she looked back at Danesh. "Thanks so much. See you soon!"

Her companion almost pushed her out the door. As he brushed past me, he gave me a puzzled glance, probably wondering why I was snickering.

I smiled at Danesh. "Well handled."

He rolled his eyes and shook his head. "Is it five yet?" He and Jerry tidied some papers, turned out the lights, and locked the door behind them.

Jerry went to the truck. Danesh said, "I'll ride with Kylie so she won't get lost."

Jerry nodded, and Danesh headed for the passenger side of my car. At least he didn't assume it was a male prerogative to drive. I got in and hurriedly cleared off the passenger seat. "You don't have your own car?" I asked as Danesh slid in.

"Sure, but we carpool. I only live a mile from Jerry."

I nodded and pulled out of the parking lot after Jerry's truck. I would be stuck in the car with Danesh for the whole drive, and I didn't know if I had that much conversation.

"How far is it?" I asked.

"Forty-five minutes, maybe."

"It's so funny. I mean, New England is tiny. You can drive across three or four states in a few hours.

But you don't have to drive across state lines just to get dinner."

"Here, you could stand in four states at once, if you're in the right spot. They have it marked so the tourists can do that."

I'd heard of the Four Corners Monument, which marked where Arizona, Colorado, New Mexico, and Utah met. I didn't want to admit that I'd thought I might like to play tourist and visit. But I wondered if I could use his mention of tourists to introduce a topic that interested me more.

I hesitated, remembering how he had shut down when I tried to tease him about the New Age crowd thinking he was a shaman, but I wanted to understand. "You get a lot of people like that girl who was just in?"

He grunted.

"I'm not surprised people assume you're Native American." I tried to think how to word my question so as not to offend. "Does that affect how people treat you in this job?"

"Sometimes." He sighed and turned toward the side window, but a few seconds later he looked back with the half smile in place. "It's very trendy in some areas to be Native American. At least to people who aren't."

"But you don't take advantage of it."

"It's cheating and it's ... shallow, I guess. For all the progress we've made with civil rights, people still have a lot of stereotypes. With Native Americans, some of the stereotypes could be considered positive. They're seen as heroic, with some sort of mystical power. But in reality too many of them struggle to get by. Anyway, I don't like to get attention for the way I look."

I could imagine women flocking to him, especially when he smiled. Most men would love the attention, but something in Danesh's voice told me he was telling the truth.

We drove in silence for several minutes, and then Danesh began to talk. "My first college girlfriend—

her name was Jennifer. I was so flattered when she came after me. And she did pursue me, one hundred percent. She was beautiful, smart, fun, with this long red hair and long filmy skirts. It took me a while to realize she thought I was Native American, and she liked that."

He sighed. "For a while... I didn't even tell her the truth. When I did, she was disappointed. She was into dream catchers and vision quests, stuff like that. She didn't want to hear about my Filipino grandmother, let alone the Danish side. I was supposed to resent whites for betraying my people. I played along for awhile, but finally I got sick of being pushed to be someone I'm not."

"Wow," I said and thought what an inadequate response that was. No wonder Danesh resented people assuming he was Native American. "But you must realize that working at a site like Lost Valley is going to make things worse. People come here with Native Americans on their minds. They might not make the same assumptions in a big cosmopolitan city, like San Francisco or New York."

Danesh gave a shudder of disgust. "It's not worth it. College in Boulder was enough city for me. I'll put up with a lot for this." He gestured at the landscape, which still seemed barren and brown to me. The rock formations were fascinating, but cool and impersonal, not welcoming.

"I was star watching once, alone up on a mesa," Danesh said. "During the Leonid meteor shower. It was mid-November—dark and cold, but perfectly clear. Amazing. I saw shooting stars by the dozens. Then it started to get foggy, so I headed back about three in the morning, through these patches of swirling mist. I came out of one of them, and standing on the path in front of me was a wolf. A gray wolf—huge! You have no idea how big they are until you see one up close. We stared at each other for a long time. I think he was as startled as I was."

He was silent for a moment. "Finally I realized I could be in danger. The wolf seemed to be waiting for me to make the first move, so I shook my backpack and it rattled, the pot and fork and tin can from my dinner, human sounds. The wolf turned around and walked away."

He grinned at me. "I can't tell you how nervous I was the rest of the way back to my car! Afraid that it might appear again... but hoping it would, too. It was the most incredible experience of my life."

"It sounds amazing." I had to force my eyes away from his smile and back on the road so we wouldn't crash. "I'm jealous."

Danesh sighed. "Jennifer insisted that it was my spirit guide. Said I should have asked it questions instead of scaring it away. But it wasn't anything mystical. It was a real, wild, powerful animal, and to me that was better. Anyway, I decided then that I wanted a job that kept me outside, not sitting at a desk all day long. So maybe the wolf was a guide, in a way."

"I like that thought."

We rode in silence for while, and then Danesh started talking about some of the other area attractions—Monument Valley, Mesa Verde, the Canyonlands. He made me want to visit every one of them, and I wondered how long I could extend this trip. I had already started looking into jobs in the region, even before I knew how I felt about it. Now I was starting to believe I could be happy living here. I might not have embraced the landscape the way he did yet, but I was starting to see how it could get under your skin.

Danesh gestured toward the road ahead. "Almost there."

A glance at the clock confirmed that we had indeed been driving for over half an hour—and it had been easy to keep the conversation flowing. I squinted at the faint bumps on the horizon. The billboards were visible first, then neon signs, and before long we passed fast food joints and motels. Jerry turned once, then again, and I lost sight of his truck, but Danesh directed me, and within five minutes of entering town we reached the ball field.

The field was a hard-packed tan diamond surrounded by a hard-packed tan landscape. It looked like someone simply put up a fence and some bleachers in the desert and painted lines on the ground. At least finding a parking space wasn't hard; cars sat at random angles behind the bleachers.

We got out to join Jerry as a tall, thin woman hurried toward him. She reached him first and gave him a quick hug and kiss. Then she turned to Danesh.

"Danny, honey!" She pecked his cheek lightly. "And who's your friend?" The way she said it suggested we were dating.

"Kylie, our visiting archaeologist," Danesh said. "This is Maureen."

I'd been wrong about makeup here. Not that Maureen was gaudy, but she was definitely wearing eye shadow, mascara, and lipstick, and I'd bet on foundation and blush, too. Her hair, brown with frosted blond highlights, was permed and spritzed into a fluffy helmet of curls. Except for the shorts and T-shirt, she looked ready for a sorority party, not a ballgame.

"Pleased to meet you." Maureen held out her hand, and I gaped at the long, hot-pink nails with little rainbows and butterflies on them. Maureen chuckled. "Oh, don't worry, they're fake. I'll probably lose one or two during the game, but I can fix them in no time." She leaned forward conspiratorially. "I do them myself."

I nodded and shook hands. I wondered if the whole team was like this. For a big city girl, I felt decidedly outshone. Maureen seemed an odd match for shy, stuttering Jerry, but as she chattered while we walked toward the field, I decided maybe they were perfect for each other. Jerry was a good listener, and Maureen obviously liked to talk.

"It'll be fun to have another girl around," Maureen said. "Danny hasn't had a girlfriend in ages. I try to set him up, but he's so picky."

Danesh gave an awkward laugh. Before either of us could speak, Maureen went on. "You'll have to come to church on Sunday. We're having a ladies' luncheon afterward, just the girls, you know. You'll get to meet everyone."

"Um, maybe...." Not.

Maureen didn't seem to notice any lack of enthusiasm. "We play softball Wednesday evening and bridge on Thursday. On Fridays and Saturdays we usually go dancing or to one of the bars, and Sunday there's church and usually a picnic or something in the afternoon."

"I'll have to see...." I said.

Danesh winked at me. "She's here to work, not get caught up in the whirlwind of local social life."

"Well, I know that," Maureen said. "I'm only trying to make her feel welcome."

I had to smile at such warmth, though I suspected Maureen's friendship could get a little overwhelming.

We joined a group of people, both men and women, mostly in their twenties and thirties but some older. Some of the women wore makeup like Maureen, but not all. Everyone greeted me warmly, and I promptly forgot all their names.

When they heard I was working at Lost Valley, talk turned to the excitement of the night before. "I heard that horrible man was released already," a woman said.

Voices rose in disagreement.

"The police are busy," the woman said. "They just had a drug bust at the high school." She leaned forward and said in a stage whisper. "And you would not believe some of the people involved!"

Talk turned toward that, but I wondered if the woman could possibly be right. Surely they wouldn't let the man go without bail, which he could hardly afford. But maybe they didn't take domestic violence so seriously out here. My stomach churned at the thought that he might be free already.

Finally the gossip died down. "Kylie is on my

team," Maureen said, slipping her arm through mine. "What position do you play?"

I'd been doing more pitching recently, but that was too public a role. "Um, shortstop is good, but if anyone else—"

"No problem! You're our guest. And I play second so we'll be right together."

Nobody else seemed offended. I cast one helpless glance back as Maureen dragged me onto the field. Jerry was settling himself on the bleachers. Two little boys had cornered Danesh and were showing off a radio-controlled car. He grinned and waved at me. I resisted the temptation to stick out my tongue at him and resigned myself to an "interesting" experience.

Twelve

By the end of the first inning, I decided I was probably one of the best players—not that skill made much difference. Players made crude but good-natured jokes about the other team and sometimes their own teammates, cheered whenever anyone hit or caught the ball, and teased without cruelty when someone missed. I was glad I hadn't mentioned pitching, because our pitcher was the best player. Grace looked about twelve, all long arms and legs and long brown hair, her serious concentration and sizzling fastball a contrast to the outfielders, two overweight guys guzzling beer and a little girl picking dandelions.

When my team was up at bat, I answered curious questions from half a dozen people, turned down a can of light beer and accepted one of cola, and hit a single before the next two batters struck out.

Three innings later, I had no idea what the score was or even if the same players were always playing on the same team. Sometimes people from the bleachers joined in when other players wanted a break; Danesh spent one inning in the outfield deep in conversation with his neighbor, and Jerry was coaxed to take the catcher's mitt for a while.

Finally, in the middle of the fourth inning, shouts from the bleachers sent everyone rushing toward home plate. I stumbled after them, wondering what was wrong. Then I noticed the pizza delivery truck. People pulled money from their wallets and handed it to Maureen, who counted it all. "We each put in about five dollars," she told me, "if you have it."

I patted my pockets and remembered that my wallet was in the car.

"It's on me." Danesh winked at me and handed a ten to Maureen.

I grabbed a piece of supreme pizza and looked for a seat. Maureen sat on the bleachers next to Jerry, her arm draped over his shoulders, chatting to someone standing nearby. Danesh was talking to Grace, the pitcher, who ducked her head shyly so her hair half-covered her face, but then laughed at something he said.

Two men converged on me. "So how long are you here for?" one asked. His graying hair and the lines around his eyes suggested middle age, but the way his blue eyes glinted suggested a bachelor on the prowl.

I'd finished classes and only had to deal with my thesis, so my time was flexible, but I kept it vague. "It depends on my research. A few weeks."

The other man said, "That's all?" He was slightly plump, with thick black hair and tan skin, no more than twenty. I thought he had a Spanish name, but I couldn't remember what.

I made a vague sound and took a bite of pizza, glancing around at the crowd. Here was another game. Everyone seemed to be flirting with someone, who half the time was flirting with someone else. Even the couples bantered with people other than their dates or spouses. A plump redhead leaned over and whispered something in Jerry's ear, causing him to blush and Maureen to playfully shoo her away.

Forget ancient peoples. This was a strange and mysterious culture.

We played a few more innings, maybe six in total, but I wasn't sure. Nor did I have any idea which team had won, though everyone seemed to be bragging and putting down the other team. Some people said goodbye and headed to their cars. I grabbed a change of clothes and a towel and followed Maureen to the women's "locker room," a box with cement floors, one shower with a trickle of cold water, and a large metal mirror. Five of us took our turns in the shower and then crowded around the mirror to brush hair and touch up makeup.

Maureen pulled a ring out of her makeup bag and put it on her finger. "There!" She held out her hand and a large diamond flashed. "I'm afraid to wear it during the game, but I feel naked without it."

"You just want to show it off," one of the women said with an envious glance.

"Is that an engagement ring?" I asked.

"Yes! Jerry gave it to me two weeks ago. Isn't he the sweetest thing?"

"Mmm." I thought the ring a bit ostentatious, but Jerry obviously understood what Maureen liked.

"He's going to make a wonderful father."

I couldn't help shooting a look at Maureen's flat belly.

She laughed. "Oh no, honey, I'm not pregnant—yet! Jerry says he has to finish paying off the ring, and then we can get married, and we'll buy a house. Something big enough for us and three or four children. I love children!"

One of the women turned on a hair dryer, which didn't stop the chatter, but it gave me an excuse to back out of the way and make room at the mirror. I wondered if Jerry knew what he was in for. Of course, on a park ranger's salary, it could take him a couple of years to pay off that ring. Maybe he'd gotten such a big one in order to buy himself time.

Finally we left the bathroom and went to join the men. Maureen linked her arm through mine as we walked toward the bleachers. "That Danny is such a sweetie pie! I'm glad he's finally found someone nice."

That was too much. "There's nothing between Danesh and me."

She shot me a sly look. "Maybe not yet ..."

"Look, he's really not my type."

One of the other women gave a husky laugh. "Honey, he's every woman's type. Look at him!"

"Looks aren't everything." But I couldn't deny the

tug in my belly as I gazed at him. He was leaning back on the bleachers, relaxed and laughing, the muscles in his arms set off by a black T-shirt, his dark hair loose and damp.

Our eyes met as I got closer, and he held my gaze with a smile that made my knees weak. I reminded myself I'd only just decided he was tolerable, but at the moment I couldn't remember why I'd ever disliked him.

Grace gave me a shy glance from her big brown eyes and whispered, "He's nice. I like him."

Everyone seemed to, for one reason or another. I thought of my ex, how I'd sometimes had to defend him to people, excusing his poor social skills as the typical male inability to read others' emotions. But not all men were the same. Why had I settled?

If the attack and losing Jonathan had one silver lining, it was giving me a chance to see what I'd really had before and what I really wanted now. I hoped I wouldn't have to cry often, but I wanted a man who would hold me when I did. Someone who'd stand by me, no matter what our future held.

Danesh rode with me to the bar, smiling and tapping his fingers to the music I had playing. I'd never seen him so relaxed. But I'd only seen him a few times, and some of those under unusual circumstances. Maybe he was like this most of the time.

He smelled good, kind of spicy, and I found myself leaning toward him slightly as I inhaled. I pulled myself back. Ignoring his total hotness had been a lot easier when I didn't like him.

We pulled up to the bar, a sprawling wooden building with beer signs in the windows. I slipped my ID and a twenty into my pocket as Danesh got out. I took a deep breath, trying to gather my wits, but it didn't help that his scent lingered.

I frowned at myself. I had to get a grip. I wasn't about to get googly-eyed over someone merely because he smelled good and looked like sin. I was in control, not my hormones or his pheromones or whatever. Enough!

I shoved the door open. It bounced back at me and I heard a whoosh of breath as Danesh staggered back from the car.

I gasped. "I'm sorry!" I tried to leap out of the car, but my seatbelt jerked me back. Heat rose in my face as I fumbled with the catch and finally made it out.

Danesh was half bent over, rubbing his knee. "I get it. You don't like guys to open doors for you. Won't happen again."

"It was an accident! I didn't see—"

He straightened and I realized he was laughing. "No real harm done—despite your best efforts."

My face burned. "It really was an accident."

"I know. Come on." He took my hand.

I jerked my hand away before I realized what I was doing. He stared at me and I had to look away.

"Kylie? Why don't you like me?"

"Who says I don't?" I mumbled.

He laughed. "Boy, do you sound guilty!"

"I don't—it's not—" I shook my head and groaned. "I feel like an idiot."

"That wasn't exactly my intention. But if you want me to keep my distance ..."

I sighed. "Look, it's not you. Really. I'm just ... I get kind of jumpy around men. It's not personal. It's like my body reacts before my brain even has time to think about it." The silence stretched as I waited for him to ask for an explanation.

"So no fast movements?"

I managed to look at him. "That would help."

I saw the familiar almost-smile come back with relief. He said, "Do you think you could manage to dance with me, with advance warning?"

I nodded. But I couldn't quite bring myself to take his hand as we walked toward the door. Dating had been easy once. I'd always felt in control. Now I struggled to even figure out what I wanted. I guess I hadn't returned to normal yet.

The bar screamed "cowboy" inside, from the customers in jeans and cowboy boots to the scuffed wooden floor left open in the center for dancing to the country music playing. I even saw some cowboy hats and giant belt buckles. The softball players had taken over one end of the big room and most already had beer. Maureen waved us over to the chairs she'd saved. I decided one beer would only keep me from driving for an hour, and I had to stay that long to be polite. I drank half of it quickly, quenching my thirst and trying to steady my nerves.

A tall man with thick, snow-white hair and a full beard bowed in front of me. "Duane Stevens. I make a point of dancing with every newcomer. Well, the ladies anyway. May I have this dance?" I nodded and he whisked me across the floor, regaling me with tales of raising horses, goats, and rabbits, and ending the dance in a deep dip that had me laughing. I was meeting more characters in one day than in a year in Boston. I was sure Boston had plenty of characters, too, but they didn't mingle as much.

Most of the softball team hit the floor as soon as they finished their first beers. I hardly had time to thank one partner before someone else took my arm. Maureen and a couple of the other women even grabbed me for some hip shaking during one rowdy rock song. I glanced at the tables and saw Danesh, leaning back in his chair with his leg stretched out. He was talking to someone but his gaze held steady on our group. I couldn't tell if he was focused on me or someone else, but I edged behind one of the other girls to hide my blush.

A catchy tune blared and the crowd roared. Those who had taken a break rushed to the floor and lined up in groups of four or five, linking arms. I ducked away and took advantage of the empty bar to get a glass of water. I downed it and limped back to the tables. If I'd known I would be dancing, I would have brought dancing shoes.

Danesh was shaking his head at a woman trying to wave him onto the floor. I collapsed into a chair and frowned at the cluster of beer bottles, which had multiplied. I'd never find mine again. In any case, I knew better than to drink from something I'd left unattended, even if it was hard to imagine danger from this friendly crowd.

"Take mine." Danesh held out his bottle.

I'd seen him drink from it, and I was still thirsty, so I took a sip.

"Are you having fun?"

"Yes." I rotated my shoulder. "Except for that one guy who seemed to think we were bowling rather than dancing, and I was the bowling ball. But otherwise, yes. I haven't danced in a while. It feels good to get back to it."

On the dance floor, the crowd was stomping and kicking in a huge circle. A few couples—to my surprise, Jerry and Maureen among them—stayed in the center of the circle, gracing the basic dance step with the addition of twirls and place changes.

"No Cotton-Eyed Joe for you?" Danesh asked.

"I know how, believe it or not. But it's been a long day, and I don't have the energy."

I handed back the beer and he took another drink. "Understandable. Think you'll have the energy to dance the next one with me?"

I smiled. "Sure, though I ought to wait until I hear the song before I commit. If it's fast, go easy on me."

"No worry there. They always follow Cotton-Eyed Joe with something slow."

"Thank goodness." Then it hit me. A slow dance with Danesh. Had the room suddenly gotten even hotter?

Thirteen

Cotton-Eyed Joe ended and the dance floor emptied, most people heading to the bar and clamoring for drinks or else stepping outside where the night air might be a little cooler. A leisurely song I didn't recognize started playing. Danesh rose and held out his hand. I felt my heart thudding as my hand seemed to rise of its own accord and slip into his. I felt like I was floating somewhere outside myself, looking down on us as he led me to the dance floor.

Then his arm slid around me and pulled me back to earth. I could feel the heat of his hand pressed against my low back, the calluses of the hand holding mine. He was a smooth lead, no fancy moves, but perfect rhythm and the right amount of pressure to guide me clearly without any suggestion of force. I remembered my swing dance teacher saying, "You don't tell your partner where to go. You ask so nicely that she wants to go where you lead." This was a perfect example.

We had the dance floor almost to ourselves, and Danesh made use of the space, leading me in lazy circles. Our eyes met and he smiled. Not his cautious half smile or the jaw-dropping full-on grin, but a friendly, casual smile that said, "Isn't this fun?" I dropped my gaze but smiled back.

He was half a foot taller than I was, but not so big that I felt overwhelmed. I was about eye level with the curve where his neck met his shoulder. I started to realize how dangerous that was when I had the urge to lean in and take a bite.

I dragged my gaze away, but looking down at his chest in the snug black shirt wasn't much better. I looked over his shoulder but started to feel rude that I was avoiding eye contact. I'd been rude enough earlier. No doubt he was watching me in that intense way he had, maybe even guessing the effect he was having on me, something I preferred to keep secret.

I forced my lips into a little smile and gave a friendly glance at his face. He was looking away, nodding to another couple as they danced past. Talk about a blow to my ego.

Why did I assume everything was about me? Had I always been this vain? Or was it another aftereffect of the attack, the self-absorption of the victim who can only see things through the lens of how they affect her? I knew I was getting better after six months of counseling, but sometimes I wondered how much farther I had to go.

My eyes suddenly focused and I realized I'd been frowning over my thoughts and staring at Danesh's face without really seeing him. And of course *now* he was looking at me, his expression puzzled and a little worried. He raised his eyebrows in question. "You all right?"

I nodded. "Fine. Really." My smile seemed fake even to me. "Just getting tired. I think after this dance I'll call it a night."

At that moment, the music ended. "I'll walk you to your car."

I glanced around, wondering if I should say goodbye to Maureen and the others, but people were already heading back to the dance floor after their break. No doubt I would see them again anyway, and I didn't want to get stuck in conversation. I was feeling lightheaded and wanted fresh air.

We walked to my car in silence. I unlocked the door and opened it, then turned to say goodbye. "Thanks."

"You're welcome. I'll see you tomorrow."

I hesitated, half waiting for something more. I wasn't sure what.

He asked, "You sure you're okay to drive?"

"I didn't have much to drink."

"No, but you're tired. It's a long drive."

What would he say if I claimed I was too tired to drive back? Would he invite me to stay the night? I didn't see anything but concern in his face. I said, "I'm feeling better already, with the fresh air. I'll put my windows down, and I'll be fine. Once I get on those washboard roads, I wouldn't be able to fall asleep if I tried."

He studied my face a moment longer, then nodded. "Good night, then. See you in the morning." He stepped away but waited while I started the car and pulled out.

I waved as I backed toward the street. He lifted a hand in response and then turned away.

I headed out of town with a strange sense of loss, like saying goodbye to friends at the end of the semester. I guess I was still more used to being around crowds of people than camping by myself.

I tossed my head, rolled down the windows, and turned up some music. One thing for sure, after a day like that, I would get a good night's sleep.

I wondered if I would dream of Danesh.

No such luck. I dreamed of hearing voices in the dark as I searched for something, but I didn't know what I was supposed to find. I woke at one point, disoriented in the pitch black until I remembered where I was. The trees rustled in a strong wind and the sides of my tent rippled with a soft flapping sound. I squirmed around in my sleeping bag and finally fell back asleep.

When I woke again the sun shone brightly and the morning chill was edging toward warm. I thought I'd slept late but discovered it was barely 7:30. I groaned and stretched my stiff muscles. Staying in bed would have been tempting if the bed were a little softer and I wouldn't be missing the best part of the day for working.

I dragged myself up, scrounged some breakfast, and gathered my gear.

As I headed out of the campground, I saw Robert West sitting at his picnic table by himself. It seemed strange to see him without Lily. I had barely exchanged a handful of words with him, ever, but when he waved I walked closer.

"How are things?" I asked. "Is everyone all right?"

He nodded. "Lily is staying in town with Amanda and the kids. At a hotel. Lily wants to keep an eye on things. But they get nervous with a man around."

"You know it's not personal." I couldn't blame Lily for wanting to stay involved. Eventually the other woman would have to take responsibility for herself and her children, but she probably wasn't strong enough yet. "Is she afraid Amanda won't press charges?"

"Fortunately, she doesn't have to. The district attorney can prosecute anyway, especially with the witnesses we have and the fact that he pushed me and damaged government property. The police are being great. The only problem is most of these folks will be heading back to other states soon. Lily and I will come back for the trial, if there is one, but they might try to plea bargain to save the hassle."

I nodded. As much as I wished my attacker had been caught, I was relieved that I didn't have to go through a lengthy trial. The thought of seeing the guy again and describing what had happened in front of people made me want to throw up. "I'll come back, too, if I need to. And let me know if there's anything else I can do to help."

I headed to the canyon, still thinking about Amanda and the children. I hadn't even known their names, still didn't know the boys' names. I didn't even want to know the man's name. I was glad Lily had taken responsibility for the family. They trusted her, and she would know where to get more help. I really did wish I could do more, but the family needed expert counseling. I doubted sharing my experience would really resonate with Amanda. Still, I took it as a good sign that I could worry about someone else for a change, maybe even imagine myself someday volunteering on a hotline or finding some other way to help.

As I headed for the storehouses, I thought back over the last few days. So much had happened so quickly that I had trouble remembering it all. But I had a nagging feeling more had happened than had been explained. Was that man really responsible for everything? The thefts, sure, and his wife must have been crying my first night. But what about the ghost lights and sounds in the canyon? What would he be doing there?

I remembered the plane and rumors of smuggling and drugs. Had he been involved somehow? I'd try to remember to suggest that to the police when I had a chance, though by now they probably knew far more than I ever would.

The morning passed quickly. I was getting a lot done, despite all the distractions of the previous days. If I finished up sooner than expected, I'd have more time to do some touring of the region. But I was finding myself strangely reluctant to leave this little community. I'd assumed I'd be on my own, but with so few people around it didn't take long to get involved.

I was sitting on a rock, drinking water and considering a lunch stop, when I heard a hello and saw Danesh coming down the path. He was wearing shorts and a light gray T-shirt that made him look very tan.

I rose and put my hands on my hips. "You know tourists are not allowed down here. Only official people in official uniform."

He grinned. "I'm hoping your sign does the trick. I have your T-shirt, by the way."

I sighed. "I was rather enjoying having an excuse not to wear it."

His gaze roamed over my snug tank top, but he only said, "How's the work going?"

"Great. Quicker than I expected. Are there any other storehouses I might not have noticed? I'll probably get the best results from the places most hidden."

"Actually, yes. You see that path that isn't really a path? It's a little tricky, but if you work your way around, you'll find another storehouse. Probably older than these, from before erosion washed away most of the path."

"Show me!"

He led the way along the narrow strip of dirt and gravel that wound along the cliff. You could barely tell this used to be part of the normal footpath, since erosion had crumbled the slope to the point where you had to carefully pick out spots large enough to place a foot.

I glanced down the slope and felt a little thrill of danger. One misstep, one spot crumbling under your feet, would send you sliding. If you did fall, you'd slide down fifteen feet of rocky slope, but then you'd stop in some bushes. Painful and embarrassing, but not deadly.

Since I was focused on my footing, I almost ran into Danesh when he suddenly stopped. "What's the matter?" I craned my neck to see over his shoulder.

"I'd swear someone's been here. The path looks scuffed. Look, a rock has been dislodged and the dust hasn't settled to fill the gap yet."

"Are you sure you're not some kind of Indian tracker after all?" The joke came out before I really considered it, and I held my breath, waiting to see if he would be offended. He gave me a long look over his shoulder, but I thought he looked more amused than annoyed. Was I actually learning to read his face a little? Or was I merely guessing with hope?

Our faces were less than a foot apart. At this distance I could see flecks of gold in his dark brown eyes. I wanted to step back, get a little more distance, but I didn't trust the path behind me. I dropped my gaze and peered around his shoulder, though I really couldn't see the path ahead. "I suppose people sometimes sneak around to explore without meaning harm."

He grunted. "They do, but I wish they wouldn't. One of these days we're going to find a body in the bottom of this canyon."

I thought of Sean coming up this path when I'd first met him. Could he be the culprit? Surely he wouldn't have gone so far, probably wouldn't even have noticed the crumbling path or thought to explore past the obvious storehouses. The tracks needn't have been fresh; in dry weather, it might take weeks for dust to settle enough to cover up marks of someone's passage. Anyway, I had already scolded Sean, so I saw no reason to mention him to Danesh—especially since that might lead to questions about why I hadn't said anything earlier, and how well I knew this guy.

He moved forward a few paces. "This is it."

I crouched to examine the old storehouse. It wasn't as well preserved as the others. Nothing remained of the clay that would have covered the opening when it was in use. Even some of the blocks had fallen or crumbled. "Wait a minute. That's odd." I pointed at three holes that pierced the face of the storehouse, small, deep holes where blocks met. "I didn't see anything like this on the others."

Danesh crouched beside me. "I haven't seen holes like that on this storehouse before. I'm sure they weren't here last summer."

"So not ancient then. But surely not natural erosion. They look like nail holes."

"Some treasure seeker messing around," Danesh muttered.

"But why? What do they gain by putting holes like that between the blocks? If they were looking for a secret compartment, surely they'd tear the whole thing down. I'm glad they didn't, and I don't see why anyone would expect to find treasure here anyway, but holes like this are completely useless."

We stared at the holes. They were hardly noticeable at a glance, but a glaring affront to the preservation instincts of the archaeologist. "Wait here." I hurried back to my gear and grabbed my backpack. I hardly noticed the danger of the narrow path as I rushed back to Danesh. I dug out a magnifying glass, crouched, and studied the holes again. Then I dove back into my bag for some tweezers and carefully plucked something out of the hole. "I'd need a microscope to say for sure, but this looks like a thread of burlap or canvas."

"Nailed to the storehouse?" His voice was more baffled than angry now.

"Looks that way. But I can't guess why. Unless ..." I held the tweezers close to my face and examined the fragment of thread, then held it against a block.

"What?"

"It's almost the same color as the rock. If it was nailed across the opening, you wouldn't be able to see it—or anything inside—from a distance. With tan canvas across the front, it would blend right in with the rock."

Danesh grunted. "Someone hiding their dope stash? Hardly worth coming down here to do that, with so many convenient places around the campground. Maybe one of the New Age gang doing who-knows-what."

I peered at the interior of the storehouse. "If anything was there, it's gone now. But if I come up with marijuana in my samples, I'm not going to assume the Ancient Ones smoked it."

Danesh managed to smile. I pondered the holes and then the voices and lights at the ruins, the note I'd found. Maybe I shouldn't keep brushing off the odd happenings.

Just as I decided to tell Danesh everything, he spoke. "How about showing me what you do?"

"Sure." It was nice of him to take an interest. I'd tell him about the weird stuff in a minute. I showed him my tools and how I took samples, and we talked about archaeology and research techniques, safe topics that almost let me forget that I was sitting next to one of the sexiest men I'd ever met.

I started to feel lightheaded, and I finally realized it wasn't only Danesh making my heart pound and the world seem off-balance. "Much as I love to talk about this stuff, I'm hungry and I'm baking out here in the direct sun." I removed my hat and wiped my forehead. Danesh wasn't even sweating. "You look disgustingly comfortable," I grumbled.

"I'm hot."

He had that right, but I kept my mouth shut.

"I'm used to it," he said. "Next time come in spring or fall."

"Excellent idea. Now I have to go collapse somewhere shady."

"I brought sandwiches. We could go down by the river where it's cooler."

I remembered the cool spray of water and felt better already. "What about Jerry?"

"He already has his. He has to stay in the office, but I'm off today, so I can do whatever I want."

That's explained why he wasn't in uniform. "So you spend your free days out here too?"

He shrugged and got up, not looking at me. "I wanted to see how you felt after last night."

He was worried about me? Checking up on me? I wasn't sure whether to be offended or touched. Or did he mean he wanted to see how I felt *about him* now? No. I had to stop reading into things. Anyway, that was a question I wasn't ready to answer.

"I feel fine. I slept well after all the exercise yesterday." I got up, too, and took deep breaths until it didn't feel like the world was spinning. I didn't want Danesh to know how badly I was feeling the heat, but I had to get out of there. "So, sandwiches by the river?"

"The Cokes should still be cold. And I got chocolate chip cookies."

Now this was a man who knew the way to a woman's heart.

Fourteen

We headed down to the cool, shady bottom of the canyon and perched on a boulder by the river. Given the size of the rock, we sat only about a foot apart, so I was glad for the distractions of views and food. I kept glancing at Danesh's hands as he ate. Strong, brown hands and forearms with well-defined muscles.

I imagined those hands running over my skin. I told myself to stop thinking about that, which of course meant I couldn't stop. Oh yeah, the libido was making up for six months of abstinence. My brain might not know what it wanted, but my body had pretty clear ideas.

One piece of good news—lusting after Danesh didn't set off any of my panic triggers. Touching might be a different matter, but at least I could fantasize.

Danesh pointed to a pair of ruined structures perched inside the canyon rim above us. "Have you looked around Twin Towers yet? From here you can see how they're built on huge boulders."

"I've only walked past. It's fascinating, though, that they built structures that follow the natural shape of the rock underneath, in addition to their usual round, square, and D-shaped buildings. It's a surprisingly diverse architectural style for a small group of people."

"They knew how to work with what they had available," Danesh said.

"But there's still so much we don't know! The Twin Towers appear to be apartment buildings—and that whole concept still floors me—but what about Round Tower?"

"You mean because there's no doorway on the first floor?"

I nodded. "They must have climbed a ladder and gone in through the roof. That sounds defensive, but we haven't found anything to suggest a warlike people—few weapons or mutilated bones."

I noticed that I had used "we," aligning myself with the archaeologists who had studied here over the years. Even though I had nothing to do with that research, I felt part of it now. "And what did they have to fight for, anyway?" I added. "Not gold or jewels."

"Water, food, resources."

"Did they have to defend the tiny spring here from neighboring bands? Or were the thick-walled towers simply an architectural style? Did they have some other use?" I shrugged and hugged my knees, feeling the bubble of pleasure that came with questions like these. "That's what I love about archaeology. Wondering, guessing, testing. We may never know for sure. Or I might make a new discovery that answers one of those questions."

"I hope you do. Have you seen the wooden lintels yet?"

"No, I've only read about them."

He rose in a smooth movement. "Come on."

Bossy. I stayed where I was. When he looked down at me, I raised my eyebrows.

He smiled. "If you'd like to take a look?"

I laughed. "Absolutely."

We hiked along the river and then headed up a steep path toward the rim. I thought I was in pretty good shape, but I was panting to keep up with Danesh. I hoped he didn't notice.

He glanced back at me and slowed. "Sorry. We can rest up here on this ledge."

Of course he'd noticed. "It's all right. I—" I took a deep breath. "Somehow I'm not getting quite enough air."

"It's the elevation. We're at over five thousand feet."

"Oh, that's right. I mean, I knew that. But I didn't expect it to make a difference."

"It's not as obvious as when you get over eight thousand feet. You'll adjust, but you might be short of breath for a couple of days."

"Whew. I thought I was out of shape."

He turned off the path halfway up the canyon wall, where the cliff formed a natural ledge several feet wide. His glance ran down my body. "You look in pretty good shape to me." He said it casually, like a fact, with no hint of flirtation, but still I felt my face heating.

"Thanks. I just—I mean, since I stopped jogging, I haven't ..."

"Why did you stop jogging?"

I winced. How had that slipped out?

My first instinct was to blow off the question, make some excuse. I didn't really want to talk about it, and he didn't really want to know. When I did talk about the attack, people got uncomfortable.

But it was part of me now, and I didn't think it was healthy for me to hide or ignore it all the time. Plus, maybe this was kind of a test. For me, to see if I could say it. For Danesh, to see how he would react.

"I was attacked." I felt like I was hearing my voice from far away. It was nothing to be ashamed of, I told myself for the thousandth time. It wasn't my fault. But I hated being a victim.

"I was jogging through the park along the river at dawn. Some guy grabbed me, dragged me into the bushes. Fortunately, someone came along walking a dog, and the dog started for the bushes, barking. The guy ran off before he had time to do much more than grope me."

I took a deep breath and gave a little shrug. I stared down into the canyon, trying to see it and not that park by the river. "I know I'm lucky. It could have been so much worse."

"You weren't lucky. You shouldn't have had to go through that at all."

"But I could've been raped, beaten, tortured ... killed, even. So many women have suffered much more, I should feel grateful—"

He interrupted. "You should let yourself feel whatever you feel. You don't need to compare yourself to anyone else. People are starving in Africa, and maybe that gives some perspective when our stomachs are grumbling, but it doesn't mean we can't feel hunger."

The counselor had told me that my fear was real and normal, that it came more from feeling powerless than from how badly I was hurt. I liked the way Danesh put it, though. I kept my gaze on the canyon below. "I guess I know that intellectually, but I still can't help feeling ..."

I didn't really want to name the feelings. But I knew I probably should. Recognizing and admitting them was supposed to be part of the process. "Stupid and weak and pathetic because I didn't fight back better. I didn't even scream—I couldn't. And like it was somehow my fault, because he chose me. And humiliated and frustrated because I let this affect me so much."

I glanced at him. He opened his mouth, but before he could speak, I said, "And you don't have to tell me that none of those things are true. I guess it didn't help that my parents kept saying, 'It's okay, he didn't rape you.' I know what they meant, but ..." I shrugged. "Even the cops told me I got off easy."

After a moment he said, "You're getting help?"

"Yes. Six months of counseling so far. It has helped. This trip is my first time away from my counselor and my friends. I wanted to prove I could be on my own, face new places and new people, especially since I'll be looking for work soon. And it's been all right. But I didn't expect ..."

"You didn't expect to need the police the other night."

I gave a short laugh. "Does anyone? I'm glad I

was there, glad I could help. Maybe it will be good for me in the long run, help me feel like I have some control."

"It can't have improved your feelings about men."

I slipped off my backpack and pulled out my water bottle. "No. You're right, I have some resentment, and it's not only because of the jerk who attacked me. The police were fine, really, only ... paternal, I guess. Lots of 'You shouldn't jog alone.' Why shouldn't I have the right to jog in a public park in broad daylight? They'd never tell a man he shouldn't go out alone."

I took a long drink. "I still get nervous around men a lot, especially if they're big or muscular, and, of course, almost all of them are big compared to me. I'm going to start taking self-defense courses, but I needed to deal with the emotional baggage first." I shrugged. "I simply want to feel safe."

"Do I frighten you?"

I thought about that. "No. I know not all men are bad or dangerous. You intimidated me at first, and I suppose that's why I took everything you said the wrong way."

"Yeah, sorry about that first day. You looked so young at first. It was like—you're going to take this the wrong way."

I turned to look at him. "Probably."

He half smiled. "I keep saying the wrong thing around you. I guess there's no reason to stop now."

"So tell me then, what was it like?"

"It was kind of like seeing my kid sister running around in the wilderness on her own. I wanted to protect you."

I snorted a laugh. "Great. What every girl wants to hear." So much for my romantic dreams. Still, the thought of him feeling protective was rather sweet, even if he was an ass about it.

His smile bloomed. "If it helps, I got over it. And I'm sorry. I didn't know about the other stuff, but now it makes sense."

When I gave him a puzzled look, he added, "Why

you went so white when I startled you. I thought it was guilt until I found out who you were. And why you were so lightheaded the next morning. It wasn't hunger, was it?"

I shook my head. I had told him more than I realized.

"And last night—I'm glad I know now."

"I don't want you to act different around me. At least, I appreciate that you call out before you get too close, but I don't want to be treated like I'm ..." I shrugged. "Fragile or helpless or something."

"I don't think you're fragile or helpless."

I turned restlessly and paced the small ledge. "My boyfriend couldn't handle it. He felt—I don't know, guilty, angry, disgusted. He wanted to pretend it hadn't happened, wanted me to ignore it, get over it. He couldn't comfort me."

"He didn't deserve you."

I smiled a little. "No. At least I learned that. We were engaged."

"I'm sorry."

I shrugged. The quick spurt of anger had vanished, perhaps for good. "I'm glad it's over. I don't want to tie myself to that kind of man." I'd said it before, but this time it felt true. I didn't miss Jonathan. I hardly even resented him anymore. I was better off without him, and I had saved myself from a miserable marriage or a tedious divorce. "I hated him for abandoning me when I needed him most. But I felt guilty, too. I felt dirty—"

He stepped close and I jumped, but when I stared into his face from inches away and felt his hands on my arms, I wasn't afraid.

"There's nothing wrong with you," he whispered.

My gaze drifted down to his mouth. I felt breathless again, but not from the altitude or the steep climb. I dragged my gaze back up to meet his. His grip gentled and his face softened. My lips parted in anticipation. Complex emotions swirled through me—gratitude, connection, nerves—but the strongest feeling of all was *want*. I leaned in.

On the path above us, gravel crunched. For a moment neither of us moved. Then his hands slid off my arms and he stepped back. I swayed toward him, my body still seeking the connection.

Someone spoke behind me, and I glanced back to see a man hiking down the path toward the river. He and Danesh exchanged a few words, but they might have been speaking a foreign language for all the sense they made to me. I leaned back against the cliff wall until I felt steady again.

The hiker went on his way, and Danesh blew out a breath. He glanced at me and half smiled. "Ready to keep walking?"

I nodded and stepped out to follow him. Had that moment really happened? My body still ached with the sexual pull. Had Danesh felt the same, or was I misreading a simple act of comfort and compassion, blown out of proportion by my hormones, overactive after six months of slumber?

I warned myself, again, not to read too much into things. I'd been wrong when I thought Danesh was a jerk and a bully. I might be wrong about this. I didn't want to develop some silly crush that might not be reciprocated.

But as I hiked up the steep path behind him, admiring how the muscles in his calves bunched and moved, I couldn't help wondering what kissing him would be like. And imagining how I might find out.

We reached the rim and hiked around to the Twin Towers. "Both doorways in this tower have the original lintels," Danesh said. "You can't really see the second-story doorway from here, but take a look at this." He crouched outside the three-foot-high, first-floor doorway of one of the buildings.

I squatted beside him and looked at the wooden lintel across the top of the doorway. Archaeologists had been able to date the buildings exactly because of those wooden beams. They could trace the pattern of tree rings, then find other trees whose rings overlapped, recording the pattern of wet years and droughts until they had a thousand-year record up to the present day. Amazing. And even more amazing to think that some person hundreds of years ago had shaped the log with his own hands and stone tools and lifted it into place above the sandstone blocks of the walls.

I closed my eyes, inhaling the scent of earth, dust, and the man next to me. I tried to imagine the building when it was new and possibly some family's home. But the vision that filled my mind had nothing to do with ancient peoples. I imagined dragging Danesh into that shady, dark space and finding out how his body felt pressed against mine.

I opened my eyes and tried to breathe. "It's ... amazing." My voice sounded husky.

Danesh was gazing up at the lintel. "It makes you feel connected to the past, doesn't it?"

I stared at his mouth and gave a murmur of agreement.

"Have you seen the petroglyphs yet, and the peepholes in Eroded Boulder House?"

I jolted. I'd never told Danesh about the lights or the map. I quickly explained. "Do you think it has anything to do with the guy they arrested the other night? Or his kids? I thought the map might be theirs, but I'm not sure if they're old enough to draw that well."

He frowned and ran his hand through his hair. "Maybe, but it's probably coincidence. It's human nature to look for patterns—that's how we get superstitions, not to mention a lot of religious practices—but just because a black cat crossed your path and something bad happened doesn't mean black cats are unlucky. I don't think we can assume that one guy or family was responsible for every weird or unpleasant thing that happened here in the last month. A lot of them maybe, but not all. That's too easy."

My legs were starting to tingle with numbness, so I stood up from my crouch. "So what should we do?"

He stood too. "I'll log the incidents, but we can't do much without more info."

I stared at the wall of the ruin, half my mind admiring how beautifully the stones fit together. But mainly I was thinking about what Danesh had said about patterns. I'd been telling myself I had to date again because I wanted companionship, sex, eventually a family. But some frightened part of me wasn't willing to trust.

I had to stop assuming that all men were dangerous and untrustworthy because one man had attacked me and one had failed to stand by me. I was taking two data points and trying to turn them into an entire theory about men. I'd allowed Sean to kiss me, as a test, but I hadn't opened myself to him as a person.

I stiffened. I had forgotten about Sean—and our date. Which was tonight. Shoot. What time was it? I had my phone in my backpack, but how could I get a look without being too obvious?

Danesh leaned against the sign describing the ruin and smiled as if he had all the time in the world. "So what made you say, 'I want to spend my life searching for relics of the past'?"

I tried to judge the time from the sun. Was it getting close to five? "Uh, I grew up in a big old house in Massachusetts, built in the 1780s. It's been renovated since then, of course, but you can still find treasures—old mahogany beams in the attic with huge square nails, things like that."

It couldn't be past four, surely. We hadn't hiked for that long after lunch. But what time had I stopped working? I smiled at Danesh and tried to focus. "When I was a kid, I started excavating outside our kitchen window. It was this old garbage pit, like they threw stuff out the window and let it sit there. I found dozens of bottles from the nineteenth century. Old medicine bottles, spice jars, beer bottles, you name it."

I was talking too fast. I forced myself to slow. "And fragments of pottery, broken tools, bent nails, all kinds of wonderful treasures. I spent my childhood digging in the dirt."

Danesh winked at me. "Most popular girl in the neighborhood, I bet."

I laughed. "I didn't have many friends. No kids lived nearby. My sister is five years older and didn't want me always hanging around. I got used to being alone."

"I can understand that. But sometimes you enjoy company now?"

He had to be flirting. I couldn't be imagining it. I could only gaze into his eyes and nod.

"So uh ... I guess ..." He glanced away and shrugged. "You're not with your fiancé. Anyone else since then?"

What had I gotten myself into? I did not want to tell Danesh about Sean. But trying to hide it seemed too risky. We hadn't made clear plans. Was Sean coming out here? He might show up at any minute and ask if I was ready for our date. Even if I met him in town, we might run into Danesh in such a small community or see someone else I'd met, who would gossip. I could try to get away from Danesh and call Sean, but I might not get through, and it would be hard to cancel now. "Well, um ... I'm not with Jonathan anymore, obviously, but there is someone—I mean it's not serious, we only had one date—not even a date, we just hung out for a while."

Danesh frowned. "If it's not serious, why are you telling me?"

My face heated, and I wanted to sink into the ground. "Because it's someone here, and I thought you might see us together. I didn't want you to be, you know, surprised."

He nodded, with no hint of a smile now. "Thanks for telling me." He rose and glanced toward the sun. "It's getting late. After four o'clock. Guess I'll stop by the office and maybe do a little gardening before I head out."

I couldn't think of anything to say, so I rose and we walked along the rim path together in silence. So that was it? It was over between us before we started? Did he think I was trying to brush him off?

I'd told him it wasn't serious. Sure, I'd managed to set up a date, and I'd only been here a couple of days—

What if Danesh thought it was somebody I'd met last night, at the softball game or at the bar? Several of the men had been flirting hard enough. I repressed a nervous giggle. What if he thought it was one of his friends? At least he knew it couldn't be Jerry, because of Maureen. At least I hoped he knew it couldn't be Jerry. But what could I say?

In case you're wondering, I didn't fall for one of your buddies last night. It was someone who picked me up completely randomly out here.

Better to keep my mouth shut. And watch wistfully as Danesh headed toward the visitors center after saying goodbye.

Fifteen

I didn't even want to go out with Sean anymore, but I didn't see how I could cancel minutes before our date. I didn't think blaming Sean because I'd lost my chance with Danesh counted as a good excuse. I checked my phone for a text, muttering, "Please cancel. Please!"

Nope. I saw a cheerful "I'll pick you up at 5!" Great. It was silly for him to drive all the way out here twice, to pick me up and drop me off, though generous, since he knew my car wasn't built for these roads. Gentlemanly, I supposed, though I didn't like being without a vehicle, in case I wanted to end the date early. I hadn't had to worry about these things in Boston, where all I needed was a subway token to get home. He'd already be on his way and probably out of cell reach. I could still tell him I'd drive myself. Would he be insulted or take it to mean I wasn't interested? Did it matter, if it kept me safe?

I blew out an annoyed breath and stomped toward the campground. I kept second-guessing myself. I hadn't been so indecisive before the attack. Maybe I was naïve before and more realistic now. But I didn't want to be a lonely old woman, peeking out from behind my curtains, spying on the neighbors and assuming the worst of everyone.

"Stop being paranoid," I muttered, earning a curious look from a squirrel. "Not everyone is out to get you."

I hurried to the restroom to clean up and groaned when I saw my reflection in the metal mirror. It couldn't have been too hard for Danesh to walk away from *that*. Washing my face and brushing my hair got rid of some of the sweat and dust, but I'd have to take that shower at Sean's place if we were going anywhere fancier than a fast food drive-through.

I realized he hadn't said where to meet. Would he come to the campground or expect to find me around the visitors center? If I waited at the office, I could casually mention to Danesh that this was the guy I'd hung out with, so at least he would know it wasn't one of his friends. On the other hand, he would know I was seeing Sean again, and that would probably lock the door that had already shut between us.

I swore to myself as I crammed a change of clothes into my backpack and made sure my wallet, phone, and pepper spray were all easily accessible in an outside pocket. This whole thing was stupid. I just needed to get through this night and then ... I had no idea what then. Celibacy was a lot easier, at least when my hormones behaved themselves, but it had lost some of its appeal. I still wasn't sure how I'd react when I got physical with a man, but my body seemed ready to find out.

It was almost five, so I headed for the campground entrance. As I passed the host site, I remembered showing Lily Sean's ID. I had already gone out with Sean once, but still, I didn't like to take off with a man without anyone knowing where I was going.

I didn't see any sign of Robert, and then I noticed that their parking spot was empty. He had probably gone into town to see Lily.

I stood in the middle of the path, wondering what to do. Leave a note at my campsite? Or here? Go to the office and introduce Sean to Jerry—and possibly Danesh?

I groaned. But better safe and embarrassed than sorry. I didn't have to ask Sean to show anyone his ID. If one of the guys at least saw us together, Sean would know there'd been a witness, and on the off chance anything happened, they'd be able to get his info from Lily.

And I was being totally paranoid and stupid. I had to stop seeing monsters behind every bush.

I stomped down the path to the visitors center. I hesitated at the edge of the trees near the parking lot, watching Danesh working in the garden alongside the building. If I was lucky, I might slip past without him seeing me. But I lingered for a minute, admiring the play of muscles across his bare shoulders, visible even from this distance. I gave silent thanks that we lived in a world where men could take off their shirts to do physical labor. At least when the men looked like that.

I sighed and crept across the parking lot to the visitors center.

Jerry stood behind the counter while a middle-aged couple glanced through brochures. I said hello to Jerry and leaned against the counter to wait. He asked about my day, and I stuck strictly to work when I answered him.

The male half of the tourist pair approached the counter. "What's the best path if you only have an hour?" Despite the fact that Jerry was behind the counter and in uniform, and I wasn't, the man was looking at me. I raised my eyebrows and turned to Jerry, who stuttered out an answer.

The man frowned and looked at me again. "Can we expect to see a lot of animals?"

I said, "I'm only visiting, but Jerry can tell you all about this area."

Jerry started to answer, but on the third stuttered word, the man turned away. "Never mind."

I glared after him as the couple left. Did Jerry have to put up with this kind of rudeness a lot? And here I was whining because I seemed to have two good-looking men interested. Talk about a reality check.

I wasn't sure if I should turn to Jerry with a sympathetic glance, say something, or pretend I hadn't noticed the insult. I felt my face heating as the moment for any natural reaction passed.

The door swung open and Sean walked in, smiling. "Hi, Kylie. Hi, Jerry. Hope you don't mind if I steal away your beautiful companion for a while."

I shot a glance at Jerry, who merely blinked mutely. I should have expected Sean to know the staff, if he came out here a lot on his days off. So much for keeping my private life private, but at least I had my witness. I quickly said goodbye to Jerry and headed out before my face could get any redder. At least Sean had parked on the side away from the garden, so we didn't have to get in a conversation with Danesh. Maybe they were friends after all!

We got in and Sean started the car. "My place first, to clean up? Not that you don't look great ..."

"Yeah, right. I won't say no to a shower. I'm not going anywhere decent looking like this."

Sean's eyebrows rose in feigned surprise. "You wanted to go someplace decent? That blows my plans."

I chuckled, though too many thoughts were rattling around in my head to really appreciate humor.

"No really, there's this great Italian restaurant, checkered tablecloths, candles in Chianti bottles, the works."

"Italian's my favorite." I doubted anything out here could compete with Boston's Little Italy, but at least it would be fun to compare.

"Then dancing. The Penthouse is pretty good. The other option is a movie, but I'd rather have you someplace where I can see and talk to you. Not to mention show you off."

It was a sweet attempt at a compliment, so I smiled. I didn't really want to be seen too much in Sean's company, though, now that I realized how small the community was. At least he wasn't planning to head back to the cowboy bar. "Do you expect to see any of your friends?" I resisted the urge to add, "and do any of them know Danesh or Jerry?"

"Maybe, but I haven't told anyone we'll be there. I want you to myself this evening."

I smiled and tried to be flattered. I had to forget about Danesh and enjoy myself. I'd had a good time with Sean before and had no reason to doubt I would again. This was my first real date in six months—actually, more like two years, since it had been a long time since Jonathan and I went on anything like a real date.

A date. My stomach fluttered at the thought. Don't take it too seriously, I told myself. It's only a date. No expectations—well, at least no obligations. Things get out of control, you pitch a fit. Worst-case scenario, you have an expensive taxi ride back out here or you get a hotel for the night. You're a big girl. You can handle it.

I tried to push the mute button on all my clamoring thoughts, turned toward Sean with a smile, and made small talk.

Sean had me laughing within ten minutes. Okay, so he didn't rev my engine like Danesh did, but he was interesting and could tell a good story. The night might be fun after all.

I recognized the route back to the edge of town, but after that we headed further into the city, if you could call it that, to what must have been considered downtown. Sean pulled up to a modern high-rise apartment that towered over most of the nearby buildings, even though I only counted six floors. An electronic gate slid back and we pulled into the ground-floor parking area, parked in a numbered space, and took an elevator to the top floor. Sean undid two deadbolts plus the lock on his door.

"You get a lot of crime here?" I asked. I only had one deadbolt on my Boston apartment.

Sean shrugged. "It doesn't hurt to be careful." With an attitude like that, no wonder he didn't blink when I asked him to show his ID. He was even more paranoid than I was.

He swung open the door and waved me in. The

temperature inside was about fifteen degrees cooler, and goosebumps popped up on my arms from the sudden change. I stopped in the middle of the large living room and looked around. He had black leather furniture, a glass-and-chrome coffee table, a TV at least three feet across, and a stereo that would have looked at home in a radio station. He did not have anything on the walls, any knickknacks, or any plants. I'm not sure what I expected, but my vision of Sean shifted slightly. So did my impression of cell phone salesmen. The job must be more lucrative than I had guessed, though no doubt living expenses were low here.

Sean said, "There's a bathroom here, but you can use the one off the bedroom and then change in the bedroom." He led the way into a room with a king-sized bed and a smaller TV and stereo. Smaller, but still way nicer than anything I'd ever owned. Maybe he had family money. Everything was clean and uncluttered. I wondered if he always lived like that or if he'd cleaned up for me.

"Make yourself at home," Sean said. "I'll be out here when you're ready." He backed into the living room, closing the bedroom door.

The bathroom was as spotless as the rest of the house. He must have a cleaning service. No man was that neat. No woman, either, unless she was getting paid for the job.

I locked the bathroom door, turned on the water in the shower, stripped, and stepped in. I shampooed twice, scrubbed at my skin, and then stood and enjoyed the luxury of hot running water. After a while, I started to feel guilty about using up that much water in the desert. Averaged over a week, though, my water usage wasn't much. When I got out, I ignored the beach towel I'd brought in favor of one of the fluffy black ones sitting on the counter.

I hated to keep Sean waiting, but it felt so luxurious to be in a real bathroom after days of camping. I'd been on the road for over a week on the trip out, mostly cleaning up at highway rest stops, and the cold trickle after the softball game hardly counted as a shower.

The least I could do was try to make the wait worthwhile. I put on the dressiest clothes I had brought with me, a body-skimming black T-dress that stopped short of my knees, and leather sandals. I didn't have a hair dryer and doubted Sean did, but I checked under the counter. No hairdryer and no cleaning supplies, either, nothing but toilet paper, which backed my theory about a maid service. With difficulty, I resisted the urge to look in the medicine cabinet. I arranged my hair the best I could, packed up my things, and stepped out to the bedroom.

Before I opened the door to the living room, I paused and took a closer look at the bedroom. The apartment seemed oddly impersonal, more like a fancy hotel suite than a lived-in home. I could understand a lack of plants or pets if he had to travel a lot or just didn't like the responsibility. But my own apartment screamed "Kylie." Books and magazines in every room, on almost every surface. Bottles from my childhood excavations on the windowsill. Photos of friends on the refrigerator. A carved wooden bowl full of fossil shells, pottery fragments, and my own badly carved obsidian arrowheads.

Sean's apartment said almost nothing. Maybe he hadn't lived there long. Maybe he really lived in a dump and had rented this place for the night to impress me. I shrugged. I wasn't planning to marry the guy; I didn't need to hunt out his secrets. I was pretty sure he wasn't the man of my dreams, but I could still enjoy the evening.

Sean stood when I entered the living room. "Wow. You look great. I didn't think there was room for improvement."

I laughed. "Knock it off. You're not trying to sell me anything."

"No, I mean it. Which makes it even harder to tell you what I have to."

I noticed that the coffee table now held a plate, a glass of water and another of wine, and three takeout containers. At first I thought he'd decided on an "intimate" dinner at home, instead of the promised Italian restaurant, probably so he could make a pass at me sooner. But then it hit me that the table was set for only one person.

Sean gave a sheepish smile. "I got a phone call while you were in there. I have to go out for an hour on business. I'm really sorry, but it's my most important client."

"I thought you set your own hours."

"Mostly, but I've been trying to set this up for ages. I didn't expect it to happen tonight, but I really can't pass it up."

I stared. He was backing out on our date now? "So what am I supposed to do?"

"Wait for me? Please?" He put his hands on my shoulders. "I won't be long. Make yourself completely at home. Watch TV, listen to music, eat dinner. I'll be back as soon as possible and we'll go dancing. I'm sorry, but I'll try to make it up to you. All right?"

"Do I have a choice?"

He laughed and leaned down to kiss me. I resisted the urge to turn my face away but didn't kiss back.

He stroked his fingers down my cheek. "I'm afraid you don't have much choice, and I'm sorry about that. But it will be all right, I promise. Don't be mad."

Easy for him to say. I could have canceled our date and stayed at the campground, but no, I didn't want to be rude. Now this. But what was I supposed to do? Insist he take me home immediately and make him miss his deal anyway? Make him pay for a cab? I hadn't even had dinner, and I was hungry. I sighed. "Only an hour, you're sure?"

"I'll be back as soon as possible. You think I'd rather be with some grumpy businessmen than with you?"

He pulled me close and leaned in for another kiss, but this time I did turn my head. "You better get going, then."

"I'll hurry." He grabbed a briefcase, winked, and headed out the door.

I threw myself onto the couch. This had to be the stupidest date ever. All dressed up and no place to go. My stomach grumbled, so I explored the food. Not bad. I hesitated over the glass of wine. I had a policy not to drink anything if I hadn't seen the bottle opened. Date rape was a lot harder to prove than stranger rape, especially when drugs were involved so the victim couldn't fight back. I was probably being paranoid again, but I pushed the wine aside and went to the sink for a fresh glass of water.

I finished the food. All of it. Sean had probably assumed that since I was little, I had a little appetite, but I'd been active all day. Served him right if he came home hungry and found nothing left.

I flipped through some of the stations on TV but wasn't in the mood for mindless entertainment. I turned it off and paced the living room. Then I started to smile. He had told me to make myself at home. If that wasn't an invitation to poke around, what was it? Maybe I'd ferret out some of his secrets after all.

Sixteen

Obviously Sean had money, which wasn't a bad thing, but the personality of his apartment had little appeal for me. Expensive toys but no warmth, nothing personal, nothing that said he had friends or family or hobbies beyond TV and video games. He seemed to have every kind of video-game console known to man, and racks of games, heavy on the world building and role-playing types.

I tried to remember the man who had talked with such interest and enthusiasm about the Southwest on our hike, but it didn't seem like that man lived here. Did that make Sean complex or had his enthusiasm been a lie? It wouldn't be the first time a man had pretended interest in a woman's work to impress her.

At first I listened nervously for any sound at the door, ready to dash back to the couch and look bored. But as the minutes passed uninterrupted, I started enjoying my role as private detective. In some ways it was like an archaeology dig—try to find clues that help you see a larger picture, without disturbing the surrounding terrain.

Unfortunately, Sean didn't give me much to work with. The bedroom, bathroom, and kitchen held barely enough to suggest that someone really did live there. Sean wore briefs in a variety of colors, with an expensively casual wardrobe on top. The bathroom medicine cabinet held three kinds of aftershave and the usual assortment of aspirin, mouthwash, and other basics. He couldn't have cooked much, given the lack of pots and pans, but he had a stack of takeout and delivery menus that must have represented every eatery within fifty miles.

I opened a door off the living room, expecting a closet. I found a small office. I hesitated, as it seemed even more invasive to investigate there, but after the way he'd abandoned me, I wasn't at my most considerate. I peeked out the peephole in the front door to make sure the hall was empty and wondered if I'd hear the elevator arriving. Then I went into his office.

Bookshelves held books on politics, probably left over from his studies, plus some true crime hard covers and rather trashy looking spy novels.

The file cabinet was locked. A safe, squatting in the corner like a metal troll, was locked. If he had personal information from his clients, it made sense to keep his records secure, but it was annoying, like not being able to get permission to excavate an area you knew had the key to your thesis.

His desk had some business cards and letterhead with his name and address, so apparently he really did live and work there. The desk drawers held only office supplies.

I considered turning on the computer, but anyone so concerned with security would no doubt have passwords. Besides, it would be hard to get a computer shut down quickly if I heard him at the door.

I sat in his executive-style office chair, staring at the dark screen. I felt like I was missing something. Well, I was missing a lot, obviously—any clue to who Sean really was.

I had a few pieces, but I couldn't put them together. How did the man who knew everything about this region and seemed to love it fit with the rich frat boy lifestyle of a luxury apartment full of gadgets and games? Why had Sean been so attentive and charming and then skipped out on our date? Was it some kind of power play, to put me off balance, to keep me dependent?

I shook my head. I was probably getting carried

away, letting boredom and my overly suspicious nature find mystery in simple boorishness.

I glanced around the office one last time and noticed a small address book tucked against the monitor. It only held a dozen entries, but then most of us kept our contacts in our phones, backed up online. I didn't see mysterious long strings of numbers or odd sounding code names, just regular names and numbers, a few female but mostly male.

I put it back with a sigh. Snooping wasn't as much fun as I'd expected. Sean was an enigma, but the biggest mystery was how he managed to keep the place so clean.

A sound came from the hallway. I froze for a moment, then dove for the office door and pulled it shut behind me, trying not to make noise. I leaped for the sofa and arranged myself casually, hoping I didn't look flushed.

Voices passed by in the hall, but the door stayed closed. I slumped back, my limbs limp as the adrenaline receded. That was probably the only thing that would get my pulse going all night. I stared at the ceiling and sighed.

A minute later I jumped up and paced the room. Sean had been gone an hour and ten minutes. I was sick of waiting. I'd go out on my own. Maybe see some of the town. I might have to take a taxi all the way back to the campground, but that was better than sitting around all night. And I wouldn't have to deal with Sean coming back all apologetic and charming, trying to salvage our date when I only wanted to be done with him. I didn't know him, didn't understand him, and didn't trust him. It was time to cut and run.

I made sure I had everything I'd brought with me. My backpack was heavy, but I didn't want to change back into dirty clothes, and the dress would look stupid with tennis shoes. I thought about leaving a note, rejected the idea, and went out. I hesitated at the door. Obviously I couldn't lock all the deadbolts, but should I leave it entirely unlocked, so I could get back in? It would serve Sean right if his expensive toys got stolen. But I couldn't imagine why I'd want to come back—if I needed a bathroom I'd find a restaurant or gas station, and I had my phone. I locked the door and headed out to explore the "city" at night.

I paused on the sidewalk and looked down the street. When I realized I was looking for Sean's vehicle, I swore. While it would be easier and somewhat satisfying to have him show up while I was leaving, so I could demand to be taken back to camp at once, I was not going to dawdle or spend the rest of the evening watching for his SUV. It was time to move on.

I turned toward the greatest concentration of lights. I passed a Chinese restaurant and then a Mexican one. A copy shop, florist, and law firm were all closed. Music blared from somewhere down the street. I saw a group of chattering teenage girls and a couple holding hands. The couple smiled as they passed.

I wasn't hungry. I didn't want to go into a bar or dance club by myself, carrying a heavy pack. The sun was heading down, but the air was still uncomfortably warm. The pack weighed down my shoulders, and my sandals weren't built for long walks.

And yet I didn't want to call a taxi and go home. If I was going to pay cab fare for a forty-five-minute drive, I wanted more from the evening than a shower.

I needed a café. Someplace I could hang out, relax, and watch the world go by, all over a latte, if they had such things here. Or maybe herbal tea, so I wouldn't be up all night thinking angry thoughts about Sean. I couldn't remember ever being treated so rudely on a date. For all my obsession over the horrible ways an evening could end, simply being abandoned in someone's luxury apartment had never entered my mind. Could it be part of some bizarre, manipulative plan? Even I wasn't paranoid enough to turn the event into a conspiracy theory, though. He was an overgrown man-child, a charming jerk who put his own needs first. Kind of reminded me of Jonathan, with better social skills when he cared to use them.

I wasn't going to think about Sean. I certainly wasn't going to slide into the cycle of humiliation and self-doubt that led to questions about what was wrong with me, what had I done to deserve to be treated that way. I knew better. I placed the blame squarely on Sean, and it would stay there. Any humiliation I felt was a side effect of anger, fatigue, and sore feet.

I paused at a fairly busy intersection and peered down each street, trying to spot a café. I needed to sit down for a while, salvage the scraps of this evening, and then find a way to get back to my campsite. I looked for a familiar Starbucks sign—surely they had Starbucks, even out here? I couldn't see one, but I'd have to cross the street to get a better angle back on this side.

A truck pulled up beside me, and its window started to go down. I figured it was some idiot going to do a "Hey baby." I subtly reached back toward the pepper spray tucked into the side pocket of my backpack and prepared to cross the street without looking at him.

"Kylie?"

I jumped and spun toward the vehicle. Sean had found me after all.

But no, it wasn't Sean.

Danesh.

Seventeen

He'd pulled his truck into the parking lane and slid across to look out the passenger window. One brown arm rested on the windowsill. The streetlights lit and shadowed the sharp planes of his face, leaving his dark eyes shadowed. "What are you doing here?"

I stared. All language left me. I found myself, inexplicably, starting to tremble.

Danesh was out of the truck in seconds. He held my upper arms, studying me. "What's wrong?"

I shook my head. How could I explain to him? I wished he hadn't seen me. I wished he would go away and forget that he had seen me, leave me to my private humiliation. But at the same time, I wanted to lean against him and feel his arms go around me.

"Where are you going?" he asked.

I managed to smile. "To a café. Is there one?"

He stared a moment longer. "I know one. Hang on." He got in the truck, backed into a parking spot, and turned off the engine. "Why don't you leave your pack here?" My shoulders ached, so I nodded and put it on the front seat. He locked the truck and touched me lightly on the elbow to indicate the right direction.

"Oh, my wallet!"

"Don't worry about it, I'll cover you." When I hesitated, he added, "You can pay me back, if you feel you need to."

He was going with me. Not just pointing the direction or even dropping me off, but joining me. Was that good or not? A few hours earlier I would have been delighted to exchange Sean for Danesh, but now my brain couldn't seem to adapt to the change. What was I supposed to tell him?

Fortunately he didn't ask questions as we walked. He greeted three people by name. One young man tried to stop and talk, frankly checking me out, but Danesh waved him off with a grin and kept walking. A minute later his hand brushed my back to turn me toward the Cactus Café.

I paused inside and stared. The place had giant blowup cacti and several bleached skulls that might have come from cows or buffalo. It also had colored lights, a small mirror ball, and oddly shaped chairs covered in burgundy or midnight-blue velvet. Weathered wooden booths were packed with chattering teenagers, while couples huddled in conversation at tiny round tables.

"Wow."

"Pretty much." Danesh guided me through the room to a table where two teenage girls were rising. "Hold the table and I'll get drinks. Tea? Coffee? Or the hot chocolate is really good."

"Hot chocolate would make this night a hundred times better."

He nodded and headed for the counter. Maybe I should have been annoyed that he'd fallen into command mode again, but for the moment I was glad to sit and get my bearings.

I saw at least three people reading and one writing on a laptop computer, despite loud, funky music. I thought I recognized someone from the softball game, and that was definitely the white-haired gentleman I'd danced with, holding a rabbit in his lap and talking to an elderly woman in a red wig.

Danesh returned with two huge, bowl-shaped mugs piled high with whipped cream topped with powdered cocoa, plus two croissants. He placed one of the croissants in front of me. "This one's chocolate. Maybe it's overkill, but you look like you could use extra chocolate tonight."

"I'll take all the chocolate I can get."

He shifted the rest of the dishes onto the table, carried away the tray, and came back with spoons and napkins. I spooned whipped cream into my mouth, watching him. He tore off a chunk of croissant and dipped it into his cocoa. He didn't speak.

I nibbled at my croissant. After a few bites, I closed my eyes and murmured with pleasure as the warm chocolate inside mixed with the flaky pastry. I opened my eyes to meet Danesh's amused gaze.

I blushed but smiled. "Thank you. I guess I did need this."

Our gazes held. He said, "Don't worry. I'm not going to ask questions."

I considered a moment and then sighed. "I'm going to tell you anyway, because unfortunately I need a favor. I need a ride back to the campground."

"Car trouble?"

"The trouble is that my car's at the campground." I made a face and forced myself to continue. "You know how I mentioned I'd hung out with someone here once? Well, tonight we had a date. Only it didn't work out."

Danesh studied me with frank curiosity. "I shouldn't have promised I wouldn't ask questions. But you don't have to explain in order to get the favor."

I laughed. "It's not that exciting, nothing to make tabloid headlines. He got called away on business. I was supposed to wait." I shrugged. "I got tired of waiting."

"Good for you. He sounds like an idiot." He leaned back in his chair. The half smile softened his face and his voice teased. "I'll drive you back. But you know, that's a long drive. You'll owe me a favor in return."

I gave him a cool look. "You could lend me your truck and ride in with Jerry tomorrow, so you don't have to give up the rest of your evening."

He nodded. "I could do that. But I'm pretty sure that service goes for even more than the ride."

I tried to keep a straight face. "All right, I'm at your mercy. You do have mercy, I hope?"

"Maybe a little." He frowned and glanced around as if wondering where he'd put it. "I'll see if I can dig it up for you. That costs extra, though."

I laughed and leaned back in my chair. The chocolate had worked its magic—and the company didn't hurt. "I'll owe you. This is a great place. Sort of like New York."

"We like to think New York is sort of like this. Actually, the owner's from Seattle. Wanted to get away from the rain."

"How lucky for people here. Do you know everyone in town? Aren't there like, five thousand people here?"

"Not quite that many. And I only know the ones worth knowing."

I settled back with my hot chocolate. "Well, tell me everything worth hearing."

If there is such a thing as a perfect evening, that must have come close. I got to gaze at that gorgeous face and listen to that sexy voice, all while sipping warm chocolate and inhaling the fragrance of coffee beans and spices. Every sense satisfied. The only thing that could have made it better is if he'd taken off his shirt, but that would have distracted me from looking at his face, so maybe it's just as well. He smiled more in an hour than I'd ever seen before, and I wouldn't want to miss that.

The place got more crowded, and finally Danesh said, "We shouldn't keep the table all night." We deposited our dishes in a plastic tub near the counter and stepped out into the night air, now a few degrees cooler. "Anyplace else you want to go?"

I looked up and down the street. I didn't want the evening to end, but I didn't feel like hitting a noisy bar or club. "Not really. I guess I've had enough of the city for a while."

What a funny thing to think, when I came from a city a hundred times bigger. But Danesh just nodded and we walked toward his truck in the soft glow of early dusk. Somehow it seemed like it should be later, but it couldn't yet be nine o'clock.

When we got to the truck, I said, "Well, what's it going to be? Are you going to loan me your truck or waste a couple of hours?" I didn't want to say goodbye yet, but it didn't make sense for him to drive me all the way out there.

"Have you ever driven a truck? Stick shift?"

I bit my lip. The only reason I even had a car was because my parents had recently upgraded and given me their old one. I never drove in Boston. "No. Look, I can take a taxi—"

He opened the door. "Get in."

"Bossy, aren't you?"

"It's part of my charm."

I raised my eyebrows. "Is that what you call it?"

He stepped closer, so I had to tilt my head back to look into his face. His chocolatey breath brushed past my cheek. "Please join me," he murmured. "I would be delighted and honored to give you a ride."

I felt my knees go weak and could only stare as his smile slowly grew.

"And if you ask nicely," he added, "I'll teach you how to drive a standard once we're on the dirt road. Then you can borrow my truck anytime you like."

I nodded slowly, not trusting myself to speak. He was a lot safer when he was being bossy. I turned and stepped up into the truck. I was so befuddled that I forgot I was wearing a dress until I felt it pull up under my rear. I quickly wriggled into place, pulling down the skirt. I glanced at Danesh as his gaze rose from my legs to my face. He gave me one heated glance that made my blood simmer, then gently closed the door and rounded the truck.

As we drove out of town, I was glad to leave the lights and noise behind. My own thoughts were noisy enough. We headed down the highway in silence, just exchanging occasional, smiling glances that brought the heat to my face—and a few other body parts. Once we left the highway for the long dirt road to Lost Valley, we rolled down the windows, and the air brushed coolly past my face. The truck wasn't as smooth as Sean's SUV, but I felt more connected to the outside world with fresh air instead of air conditioning. And I felt more alive with Danesh than I ever had with Sean. Sean had helped me prove that I could kiss a man without panicking, which was good to know, but it hadn't rocked my world.

I had a feeling a kiss from Danesh would shake the foundations. I let myself linger over the fantasy, prepping my body to react with pleasure, not panic, as I imagined his hands roaming over me.

He pulled to the side of the road. "Ready?"

"What?" I gasped.

"Do you want to drive?"

"Oh. Right." I nodded and got out, hoping the fading light hid my blush. I paused to gaze at the landscape, endless miles of desert and distant mountains. An orange glow traced the horizon, and the clouds overhead reflected an odd pale magenta.

"You might regret camping tonight," Danesh said as he passed me to switch places. "Looks like we could get some rain."

Far from worrying me, the thought of a rainstorm sent a lovely tingling across my skin. That would be an experience for sure, to be in the middle of the weather instead of tucked away safely in a cozy apartment. Whenever a big storm hit, I had this wild urge to dance naked on a cliff top somewhere. Here, I could actually do that—or at least stand outside my tent, clothed, and feel the rain come down. I didn't think I was ready to give in to my odd whim yet.

I got into the driver's seat and buckled my seatbelt. "I'll be all right. The rain fly is waterproof. If it gets really bad, I'll sleep in my car."

Danesh looked over and his teeth flashed in the faint light. "Are you sure you're a city girl?"

I smiled and settled back into the seat, for some reason absurdly happy.

Eighteen

I wasn't surprised, now, to discover that Danesh was a good teacher, patient and calm even when I ground the gears or lurched the truck. By the time I pulled into the visitors center parking lot, I felt halfway comfortable with the stick shift. And I loved driving a truck—for once I towered over everything else.

I put the truck in park and turned it off. "Whew! That was fun, thanks."

"Nice work," Danesh said.

I wondered if it would be weird to invite him back to my campsite for a nightcap—and what I might have that could possibly constitute a nightcap. My stomach jumped at the thought of getting romantic, but other body parts were demanding attention, too. I wanted to know what it would feel like to kiss Danesh, to feel his embrace. I needed to take things slowly, and I felt confident now that Danesh would understand. I'd told him about the attack and about my foolishness with Sean, and he hadn't looked down on me or backed away. I thought I could tell him anything and it would only bring us closer.

I saw now how lacking my other relationships had been. I'd assumed relationships required compromise, and they did—but I'd compromised too much, too often, without getting enough in return. I'd fallen for the conventional wisdom that men didn't talk about their feelings, that a woman could only guess and assume and interpret what a man felt or needed. I wanted more, and I thought I could find it with Danesh.

I turned toward Danesh with a smile, but he was looking at the visitors center. I'd been too focused on driving—and then on romance—to question the light on inside the building. The sky was nearly dark, just a moody red glow hanging low on the horizon. Hours after closing time.

Danesh nodded toward another truck in the lot. "Jerry is still here. I wonder what's up."

I said in a spooky voice. "Maybe the ghosts have him. Or the aliens!"

He chuckled. "Guess I'd better check. You want to come in?"

I hesitated. Jerry had seen me leave with Sean. If I came back with Danesh, would he ask questions? Would he ask mention Sean if Danesh came in without me and said he'd given me a ride? Or would they get distracted by whatever problem had kept Jerry here late and forget all about me?

I decided if any questions were asked, I'd rather not be there. In any case, nothing would happen with Danesh while Jerry was there. I seemed destined to fail at having a romantic evening. "No, I guess not."

We got out of the truck and met at the front of it. "Thanks for the ride," I said. "And the driving lesson."

"My pleasure."

We gazed at each other for a long moment. The faint light spilling from the visitors center window highlighted one side of his face, tracing the high cheekbone and strong jaw. His lips curved, and his dark eyes seemed filled with promises.

Wind ruffled my hair and caressed my cheeks. I felt a charge of electricity in the air—or maybe it was only in me. The night seemed touched with magic, full of possibilities. Nerves tingled along my skin as I held his gaze and said, "I guess I owe you. Unless you've decided on a payment?"

He gave a husky chuckle. "Better not ask that now."

I took a quick breath and stepped forward to

close the gap between us. I lifted a hand to his chest and smiled up into his face. "Well, then, here's a tip."

He dipped his head to meet me as I rose up to kiss him. Our lips brushed, retreated. His arms went around me, pulling me close. I slid my hands over his shoulders and met his mouth. One of us moaned with pleasure, I wasn't sure which. Maybe both.

The world spun in lazy circles, as if we were dancing to music from the stars. Then a warm hand slid over my hip and pressed me tight against him. My legs went weak, and I knew I'd sink to the ground if he didn't have a hold of me.

I slid my hand into his hair, wanting to pull him even closer. He shifted the angle of his head and deepened the kiss. I felt like I was being devoured, and I wanted to wrap myself around him and never let go.

He eased back and brushed feathery kisses across my lips, then planted a warm, firm kiss to my cheekbone and let out a faint sigh. He loosened his grip, making a little space between us, his hands sliding to my hips. I was glad he didn't let go, since I wasn't sure I could stand without help. I dragged my heavy eyelids open and rubbed my lips together, still tasting him. "Wow."

He laughed. "You can say that again. I've been looking forward to that for a long time."

"You've only known me for three days."

"It seems like much longer. Can I assume this other guy is out of the picture?"

"What other guy?" I smiled. "He was never really in the picture, no more than a way of passing some time. I found a much better hobby."

He drew me close again, but gently, and I snuggled against his shoulder with a murmur of pleasure. His hand brushed down my hair, and he kissed my forehead. "I'm looking forward to doing this again sometime soon."

I rubbed my cheek against his shoulder, then nipped lightly at his neck right above the collarbone and felt him tremble. "But not tonight?"

"It's raining."

"It is?" I turned my face away from the protection of his body and felt a drop hit my cheek. "I guess it is."

"I don't think we'll get a big storm, probably just a little drizzle, but you'd better get tucked away inside your tent and make sure everything is covered up."

I sighed. That sounded practical, but I didn't feel practical. I didn't want to back away. How could he? I swallowed and forced myself to speak. "Are you backing off because of what happened to me?"

"You mean the attack? Partly. But that's only one reason I want to take my time with you. You're special, Kylie. This is special. We don't need to rush."

I looked up into his face, saw the way his eyes caressed me, the way his lips curved in a smile that left me weak with desire and strong with joy. I felt something shift in my heart as a lock I hadn't even known was there broke open, and suddenly I had more room to let him in. But he was right—this was too important to rush. I smiled back at him. "So what are you doing tomorrow night?"

"I don't care, so long as I can do it with you."

I laughed and rose up onto my toes, squeezing him tight. "Then I guess I can let you go tonight."

"I'll drive you to the campground. Unless you'd rather sleep on the sofa in the office."

I eased back from him. "No. The campground is fine, and I can walk. You go ahead and check on Jerry and get out of here before the road gets muddy."

"I can walk over with you."

I kissed the corner of his mouth. "And we both know that will delay you a lot longer than the time it takes to walk. We'd better say goodbye now, or I won't want to say goodbye at all."

He cupped my cheek in his hand, warming my chilled skin. His thumb brushed over my cheekbone. When he dropped his hand, I could still feel the heat. "I'll see you in the morning," he said. "Come by for coffee?"

"Absolutely." My body still yearned for him, straining forward without conscious thought, but I knew a step back was a good idea. We had time to get to know each other, to explore each other slowly. Maybe someday I'd want to make wild love on a truck tailgate with the rain pouring down—maybe my body wanted that now—but I knew that for this first time I needed to feel safe and comfortable. Danesh was right. We didn't need to rush.

We kissed again, slowly, tenderly, full of promise. The sizzle of sexual desire eased to a languid comfort, my limbs and eyelids heavy, so I wanted to snuggle up and go to sleep. His hand stroked my back, and I almost purred.

Finally we stepped back. He glanced at the path through the woods. "You're sure—"

I laughed. "I'm a big girl, remember? And I'll be insulted if you act like it's safe for you and not for me. My eyes have adjusted to the dark. I think I'll walk along the rim trail, though, where it's more open. Then I'll have the lights at the campground to show the way in."

"All right. Be safe. Goodnight."

I smiled and waved as I headed for the canyon rim. The breeze whipped my hair around and danced over my skin, raising goosebumps, but it wasn't really that cold. A drop of rain hit my forehead and another hit my arm. Maybe I would have that chance to dance on the cliff top in a storm after all. Wouldn't that be something to tell Danesh in the morning?

I stopped at the canyon rim. The wind murmured in the trees behind me and made a low whistle as it rushed past the walls of the nearest ruin. The sky was almost completely dark now, just the faintest hint of red on the horizon glowing against black clouds above. I could barely see the looming silhouette of the ruined walls, mysterious and slightly threatening.

I tossed my hair back out of my face and grinned into the breeze. I wanted to see this place at all times of year, in all weather. I wanted to explore its secrets.

I wanted to belong.

"I could be happy here," I whispered. Danesh was part of that, part of the possibilities, but that wasn't all. I had been drawn into this world, and I wanted to stay. I was glad I had trusted the instinct that had me exploring job possibilities before I even visited.

I walked slowly along the rim path, feeling part of something larger than myself. The air smelled spicy and alive. The trees rustled and shuddered on my left; the canyon dropped away on my right, a black pit. A jagged shape loomed up, a deeper black against the darkness. Another one of the ruins—Stronghold House, the one crouched atop a huge boulder right inside the canyon rim. As I walked closer, I remembered the crevasse that separated the boulder from the rim trail. I'd have to watch my step, not get fooled into thinking the trail went closer to the ruin.

A light flickered ahead. I stopped and shook my head, wondering if staring so hard had affected my vision. I squinted and saw nothing. Just my imagination? Or somebody else out on this wild night—someone smart enough to bring a flashlight?

Where had he or she gone, then? Maybe the person had stepped into the trees or was farther down the trail and had passed behind another ruin. I waited a moment but saw nothing.

I shrugged and walked forward. Why shouldn't someone else be out enjoying the night, as I was? Maybe I wasn't the only one feeling a bit crazy.

Drops of rain splattered my skin in fours and fives now. Unless I really was going to dance in the rain, I should get back to my tent.

Voices whispered on the breeze. I paused, listening. The wind, surely—but such a human sound.

So what if it was human? Maybe two people had come out with a flashlight to see the canyon at night.

I had no reason to worry. I tried to ignore the prickles along my skin, blaming them on the chill breeze. The voices came again, faint and ghostly. I wouldn't have minded the whispers so much if I could see someone, but the vague sounds were unnerving. Like someone was hiding.

I shook my head. That was my own paranoia. Rapists might choose secluded areas for their attacks, but not this secluded. You wouldn't set up an ambush where you might not see anyone pass by all night. If people were out, they were probably ghost hunters or New Age spiritualists or storm lovers. I should find them and make sure they weren't planning to go into the canyon.

I strained my ears but heard nothing but the wind. I took a few more steps, squinting into the darkness. Shapes were flat and blurred in the drizzle, without edges or depth. I shivered and wished I had a sweatshirt, or at least jeans and real shoes.

My backpack—I'd left it in Danesh's truck. I paused, half turned back. I hadn't heard his truck leave, though I might not with the wind. I could go back for my pack and mention that I thought someone was in or near the canyon. It was really his responsibility, not mine.

I imagined myself explaining. "I thought I saw a light and heard voices, but then I didn't." Would he think it was some ploy, playing the damsel in distress? Would it add an awkward epilogue to an evening that had ended so well? Would I get over there to find Danesh and Jerry gone and have to walk back on my own again?

I stood on the path, hugging myself for warmth as the cold wind blew past my bare legs. Go forward, go back, run for my campsite? I took a deep breath and blew it out. Why had I gotten so indecisive?

Forget the question. I knew why. But if I didn't want to be a victim, I had to stop acting like one. I couldn't go running for help or hiding in my bed every time something freaked me out a little. I couldn't give men all the power, the power to scare me and the power to protect me. Both made me weak.

It was a tourist out at night, no monster or ghost or alien. No rapist lurking in the bushes in the off chance I'd wander by. I would investigate, deal with the situation should there be any need to do so, get help if I couldn't handle it alone, and then go make myself a hot drink before bed. I refused to be scared away from a place I enjoyed, a place I wanted to work and tour.

"Pull up your big-girl panties and deal," I muttered.

I walked forward. A sudden break in the clouds let the moon shine through. Falling House seemed to jump out of the darkness, a jagged silhouette of broken walls dark against ghostly clouds.

And then I saw something else—a wooden board, like a bridge, set across the gap between the canyon rim and the base of the ruins.

Nineteen

I stared at the board, wondering why on earth somebody would put it there. To get to the ruin, obviously, but why? Who would be out exploring the ruins on a night like this? Granted, they'd be less likely to be caught after hours, with the staff gone—

And then I remembered Jerry. Surely his unexpected presence and the board's were too much to be coincidence. Maybe he'd received a last-minute report of some kind of damage. Maybe he'd gone home on time and then been called back here by some complaint from Robert. Or maybe someone had requested special permission to go out for sunset photos and Jerry had arranged it.

I put a hand over my mouth to cover a giggle. Or maybe Jerry and Maureen had come out here for some hanky panky in a romantic, if peculiar, new location.

And Danesh would be waiting at the visitors center and wondering what had happened to Jerry.

I hesitated again. Go tell Danesh what I suspected? He'd probably want to come see for himself. If it was Jerry and Maureen, we didn't need to disturb them, but if it wasn't ... well, it would be better to be sure.

I turned toward the visitors center and then swore. Why did I have this instinctive reaction to turn to a man for help? Danesh would probably like it, but that wasn't a pattern I wanted to start. I was a perfectly capable, grown woman. I was tired of living in fear and letting men control my actions, one way or another. I could quietly take a look on my own. I wouldn't try to tackle a gang of rock thieves singlehandedly, but I could at least look before panicking and running for help.

I put a foot cautiously on the board. I'd just sneak across and listen long enough to confirm my suspicions. I really did not want to hear, let alone see, anything explicit between Jerry and Maureen, but I didn't see a better answer.

The board seemed sturdy enough, and if it had held Jerry's weight, it would hold mine. I took another cautious step out. Just a few more to go.

The moonlight vanished like a light going out. I froze, my arms out to the sides. With no visual frame of reference, I had a sudden sense of vertigo and swayed. I bit my lip and concentrated on the feel of the board beneath my feet. I was almost thankful for the thin sandals that let me feel the board's slight curve from my weight.

I knew two or three more steps would get me across. It didn't make sense to stand here balanced over this chasm and wait for the moonlight to come back. Turning around or backing up would be even more dangerous. I had to keep going forward.

My back foot rasped against the wood as I slid it forward. When I had it firmly planted in front of me, I moved my other foot. Three more steps and I felt my foot slide over the end of the board so my toes touched rocky ground. I edged forward, resisting the urge to hurry—I didn't want to knock the board out of place by jumping off it.

A fine layer of grit crunched under my sandals as I stepped onto the boulder. I held my hands out in front of me, and finally my fingers touched the rock wall. I blew out a breath as my heart pounded. This evening was certainly having its ups and downs.

As my nerves settled, I realized I could hear voices. A man's voice, I thought, and then—another man? I couldn't catch the words, but one voice sounded vaguely familiar. Not Jerry and Maureen, then, but maybe Jerry here with someone else?

I hesitated again, afraid to interrupt when I

didn't know what was happening. But I still needed to confirm that Jerry was here and nothing was wrong. I'd come too far to turn back now. It would be easy enough to hide in the dark, so I wouldn't let them see me until I knew for sure who it was.

I'd never been inside these ruins, but I knew Falling House had been an apartment building with many rooms. The men must not be in the first room, or I'd be able to hear them better. I brushed my hand lightly along the wall.

I remembered how low the doorways were and dropped my hand lower on the wall. When I found empty space, I crouched at the doorway, peeked through, and saw absolutely nothing.

I slipped into the room, probing with each foot so I didn't kick fallen blocks. The ruins had no roof, and the walls had crumbled in various states of decay. If someone shone a light from another room, they might see me. But the night stayed black.

I found another opening and gently felt to make sure it was a doorway and not a spot where the wall had crumbled. When I was sure, I crouched and shuffled through, wishing again I had jeans, so I could kneel. Light flashed and I jerked back. Fortunately the wind covered my quick intake of breath. The light came from the room next to this one. Someone had a penlight, and as they moved slightly, it spilled through a wide crack between the two rooms.

I edged closer, confident that if I stayed to the side they wouldn't be able to see me even if they turned the light in my direction. When I got close enough I peered through the crack.

The penlight shone at the ground, but the light spilled enough to show the bodies of two men hovering over it. No, three men—one crouched and holding the light, one leaning against the wall, and one standing, speaking and gesturing with his hands. Even in the dark I recognized his voice and the way he moved.

Not Jerry. Sean.

"Can we go now?" Sean said. "I've got business to finish."

The man by the wall said, "I know, we were late, you've told us. It's not easy crossing the desert and then finding your hiding spot, and we lost that stupid map stumbling around in the dark the other night. If you want my opinion, you're trying to be too clever. You get a kick out of meeting here because it's weird. We'd be better off at some random spot in the middle of nowhere, or even in a crowded city where no one would pay attention to strangers. You're not impressing anyone."

"All right, all right," Sean said. "Let's not argue. You're here, you got the money, now let's go."

The crouching man said, "Fine. This run has taken far too long."

I stretched up enough to see that his penlight was shining down into a briefcase filled with stacks of cash. If anyone had looked my way then, they probably would have seen the whites of my eyes as I stared. It was like flipping through TV channels and coming across an old gangster film right in the middle. My mind scrambled to make sense of it all.

"I had to make sure the stuff was good," Sean said. "Last time your boss tried to cheat me."

"Whatever." The crouching man stood. "Let's get out of here. Next time keep it simple. No games, or we're through."

He turned and the light turned with him. I jerked back, tremors skittering over my skin. I still wasn't sure what I'd stumbled across, but I knew I shouldn't let them find me here.

No way could I get back through the first room and out of sight in time. Already I could hear them muttering in the next room, slowed only by the challenge of getting three people through safely with one small light.

My instincts screamed danger, and this time I listened. I dropped to the ground in the corner and curled in a ball, trying to hide my bare arms and legs under my body. I shook my head so my hair fell over my face and neck and I squeezed my eyes shut tight, as if that would matter with my face buried. At least my dress was black and my hair dark brown.

Pebbles pressed into my bare skin, and the damp earth felt cold and sticky. A fallen block jabbed my rib cage. I tried not to breathe as faint footsteps and the rustle of clothes moved past me. I thought I heard a tap of footsteps on wood. A scraping sound. Then nothing but silence.

I started to breathe again, slow, controlled breaths that still sounded too loud to my ears.

I couldn't bring myself to look up. I had this horrible feeling that somebody was standing over me, waiting. Logically I knew that if someone had spotted me, hiding wouldn't make him go away now, but still I had to force myself to lift my head and open my eyes.

I saw only darkness.

I sighed, and the trembling started. I still hadn't quite processed what was happening, but whatever those men were up to, they wanted to keep it a secret. I huddled, hugging my legs, and tried to put the pieces together. Sean was trading money for something else. I remembered the plane flying over and the news report of a possible drug drop. Could I really have stumbled into that? And Sean was involved up to his eyeballs.

I remembered his questions about where I'd be working and his warnings about staying away from the canyon at night. Now I knew why he hadn't come back to me in an hour. The whole plan had been to get me away from the canyon that evening. He knew I was keeping an eye on things, and he wanted to get me out of the way. The old saying was true—just because you're paranoid doesn't mean someone isn't out to get you.

What an idiot I'd been not to see it sooner. Though really, who would expect to get drawn into such a thing? Here, of all places? Maybe I had decided that Sean was odd, but a drug runner? That hadn't occurred to me. Maybe because I was too wrapped up in myself to guess that his manipulations really weren't about me at all. Or maybe because "Things like that don't happen to people like me."

Well, it had happened now, and I had to get out of there and notify the police. I was still trembling, but I forced myself to move. I had to get to the visitors center and hope Danesh hadn't left yet. If he had, I needed to get into the building so I could use the phone—wait, was the key in my backpack? Darn it. I might have to drive somewhere where I could get cell reception.

I made my way through the next room and outside. It was still too dark to see, so I crawled forward and felt with my hands for the board.

It was gone.

Twenty

Of course the board was gone. They wouldn't leave it behind. They should have taken it with them when they went inside the ruins, so no passersby would notice it, but they'd sounded impatient, and of course they hadn't been expecting passersby at night in the rain.

A large raindrop hit the tip of my nose. I hadn't been paying attention to the slight drizzle, but now my predicament sank in. I was stuck on this boulder in the dark, wearing a dress and sandals, with cold wind blowing and rain falling. I might survive the night like this, but I certainly wouldn't enjoy it.

"Idiot," I muttered. "When your instincts say get help, listen!" I'd taken independence and overcoming fear a step too far. More like five steps too far—five steps across that board.

I huddled back near the wall of the ruin. The wind gusted, numbing my skin. I could yell for help, but who would hear? I was a quarter-mile from the visitors center and even farther from the campground, and people wouldn't be hanging around outside on a night like this. I might even call back Sean and his buddies. I guessed they were headed out of the park already, but my guesses so far had not been too accurate.

I could wait a while to make sure they were gone and see if the rain stopped. But the rain could as easily get worse, and the temperature would keep dropping. And the more time I took to notify the police, the harder it would be for them to track down the criminals.

I figured I had two choices. Plan to spend the night or get out of there on my own.

Clouds scudded across the sky, and a little moonlight slipped through. I looked at the gap between the boulder and the rim and immediately discarded any idea of jumping. In daylight, in running shoes, with enough room for a running start, I might make it. But right now any attempt would lead to disaster.

I peered into the crevasse, trying to judge how deep it was and how rough the sides were. I'd seen it earlier, of course, but I had only been admiring the dramatic impact, not studying it with an eye to rock climbing.

I thought the crevasse was about fifteen feet deep. At least that was better than the other side of the boulder, where if I slipped, I'd keep falling down the whole slope into the canyon. And the crevasse narrowed at the bottom, so I might be able to reach across and brace myself on the other wall once I got partway down.

I remembered the way the Ancestral Pueblo People had often cut notches into the rock to use like ladders. They had never looked like great ladders to me, especially after seven hundred years of erosion, but they might help. That is, if the Ancient Ones had done that here instead of using wooden ladders, and if I could find the notches.

I pushed damp hair out of my face and peered into the crevasse. In the dim light, I couldn't make out anything definite. And the light might disappear altogether if I didn't hurry. I reached my hand down and felt around for a notch or other foothold. I slid my hand over the rock and finally found a slight scooped-out area. I pressed my hand into the depression. I couldn't imagine standing with my weight on that, but maybe it was better than nothing.

I sat on the edge of the boulder and felt the cold rock gritty against the backs of my calves. Maybe bare feet would give me a slightly better grip than floppy sandals. I'd want my sandals once I got down, though, so I stuck them in the front of my dress. Ick. Nothing like cold, damp, mud in your cleavage.

I rolled onto my stomach and forearms, dangling my legs. My feet must be already hanging below the notch I'd felt, but hopefully it indicated a line of notches all the way down. I slid my bare feet over the damp, slippery rock.

My heart thudded and my arms strained to hold me. The dark maw of the crevasse seemed determined to suck me down. What was I doing? Was I crazy?

Finally I felt something, a rough bump on the rock. I squeezed the front of my right foot onto it and tried to grip with my toes.

I eased myself down lower, so I was chin level with the top of the boulder, still gripping with my hands and putting weight on my forearms. I searched with my other foot.

Nothing. I should pull myself back up.

I wasn't sure I could.

My left arm started to slide toward the edge of the boulder. I whimpered and gripped harder, trying to hold on even with my chin.

My left foot wasn't finding a single hold. Finally, in desperation, I jammed it onto the same bump where I had my right foot. That supported my weight enough so I stopped sliding.

I tried to take a deep breath, but the boulder pressed into my chest and chin. I doubted I could get back up again without decent footholds. I had to keep going down. If the crevasse was fifteen feet deep, and I was five feet tall, I only had ... a ten-foot drop. What was I thinking? I should've stayed on the boulder and screamed. Waited for morning if I had to. Forget independence, playing the damsel in distress was starting to sound good.

Too late now. Since my left foot hadn't found a hold, maybe I could leave it on the bump and search more to the right with my right foot. I slowly lowered my right foot, feeling with my toes. I found another notch, but with such a shallow slope that I didn't see how it could take my full body weight.

I could do this. I could.

My chin slipped off the edge of the boulder. I tried to dig in my fingertips, but with only a little dirt over solid rock, I couldn't get a grip. My arms started to slide. I would have to try the foothold because I was running out of options.

I jammed my foot in so hard my toes hurt. My other foot was starting to cramp from gripping its little shelf. I let my forearms slide off the top of the boulder and turned my hands to grip the edge of the rock with them.

I'd never felt heavier, never felt gravity so strongly, but for the moment I held on. I moved my left foot down and tried to feel around.

My hands slid toward the edge of the boulder.

I fumbled frantically with my left foot. And then I felt myself falling.

As I peeled away from the cliff, I kicked my left foot back. It hit the wall on the opposite side of the crevasse with a thud that shot pain through my heel and shook my whole body. I pressed my foot hard against that wall and pushed my right foot and hands against the wall in front of me. The good news was, I wasn't dead yet. And I was closer to the ground, though not close enough to jump safely. I was in a deep lunge, my hands trying to cling to smooth, slick rock.

My hips started to ache with the tension. Another minute and my muscles would cramp. I was afraid to move, but I had to.

I wriggled my left foot down a little. Braced my hands against the boulder. Pushed back, holding my weight between my hands and the foot behind me.

Lowered my right foot. Found another foothold.

My right quad started to cramp. I needed to shift out of this lunge, and quickly.

I could do this. It didn't have to look pretty. I just had to survive.

I turned my body slightly and swung my left hand

over to the wall behind me. My fingers brushed something feathery. I stretched and gripped a bushy plant, hoping its roots were tough and deep.

I wobbled, shook, trembled. But half a minute later I was still upright, my body stretched across the crevasse like an X.

I felt better with four solid points of contact. I edged one hand down, then the other. Then my right foot, looking for another notch. I found one, and it wasn't bad with my weight pressed into the wall instead of dragging me down.

Wisps of hair dangled in my eyes and dripped water down my cheeks. My hands stung, and my feet throbbed even though they were going numb. My hip muscles screamed with pain. My dress, stretched tight across my thighs, would never be the same. And I was getting a wedgie.

I had to ignore it all. I worked my way down the crevasse, sometimes sliding and catching myself a few inches down. Finally my feet hit bottom. My body didn't seem to understand that I'd reached solid ground. I kept going down until I slumped into a heap among some prickly weeds.

I had made it. I was drenched, muddy, and sore, but I'd gotten off the boulder.

Unfortunately, that was only the beginning. Now I had to get help and stop Sean.

Twenty-One

I huddled on the ground, dragging in deep breaths. I didn't want to move. Wasn't sure I could.

I started shivering. I had to get out of there. I could move, because I had no choice. I would do what had to be done.

I pulled my sandals from my dress and slipped them onto my feet. They weren't much protection, but better than nothing. At least the snakes would all be hiding from this weather. Loose rocks were a bigger threat.

I stood and got my bearings. I'd pretty much already exceeded the extent of my rock-climbing abilities, so I wasn't going to try climbing up the cliff to the rim at that point. But the storehouses, where I'd done my work, weren't far away. I could take the path up from there.

As I stumbled over rocks and pushed past bushes that scratched my legs, I remembered seeing Sean that first time. He must have been down at the storehouses picking up something from his drop point. And then he had flirted with me to distract me. His interest in my work had been a way of finding out where I would be working and where it was still safe to meet his partners or stash his goods. What a fool I'd been, worrying about completely the wrong things. Well, I'd pay him back. I might be a fool but ... but ... I couldn't think of a good "but."

I might be a fool, but so was he! I'd made a mistake. I could learn from it and move on. We'd see who laughed last.

I slithered along the slope, stubbing my toes on

rocks. A yucca caught my skirt and ripped it, leaving a stinging scratch across my thigh.

The slope got even steeper. I had to work my way down farther. I slid, grabbing onto bushes and trying to brace my feet against rocks when I could find them. Finally I slid onto a ledge barely wide enough so I could stand up. I kept one hand on the slope and peered into the night. The darkness flattened the scene, making it hard to judge distances. Shadows could have been dark objects or empty space.

Finally the scene clicked into place, despite the darkness. I'd come farther than I had realized. I was already on the narrow path that led past the storehouses. I stumbled along it. My skin felt numb and my muscles sluggish, like my brain was giving commands but my body was half asleep and barely listening. The wind rushed past, but at least Danesh had been right about the rain, which stayed at a modest drizzle.

I turned up the steep slope to the rim, panting from the exertion even though I wasn't going very fast. I needed to get dry and warm. I made it to the top of the slope and turned down the rim trail. I imagined wrapping up in a blanket—or even better, Danesh's arms. I used that as motivation. The faster I moved, the sooner I'd get there, and the more likely I'd catch Danesh. He could warm me up, and we could call the police right away. Although I felt like I'd been struggling for hours, it probably hadn't taken more than ten minutes to get out of the canyon. If the police had a car close enough, they might catch Sean as he left the park boundaries.

If the visitors center was closed and locked, the situation got more complicated. I'd have to get to my camp and check for the key. If I couldn't find it, I'd have to drive somewhere where I could get phone reception. Sean would be long gone before I could get help. Of course, I knew where he lived, but unless they found him with the drugs on him, they wouldn't have much of a case.

I thought I saw a small light in the distance, half hidden behind the screen of trees. A beacon of hope or merely wishful thinking? Finally I turned a corner and got a clear view. A small square of light, surely the visitors center window. Someone was still there! The light, with its promise of warmth and companionship, called me. But what if Danesh was ready to leave? I could still miss him.

The thought renewed my energy. I ran.

When I turned into the parking area, I slowed so I could drag air into my lungs. Danesh's truck was still there. Everything would be all right now.

My legs trembled with cold and fatigue as I staggered the last few paces to the door. I fumbled for the door handle with numb fingers. My trials were almost over. I pushed. The door didn't budge. I stared at it, baffled and insulted. Then I realized the obvious—the visitors center wasn't open, so Danesh had locked the door behind him.

I started pounding and didn't stop until the door opened. Then I stumbled through into Danesh's arms. Over his shoulder I could see Jerry staring at me from the doorway to the back room. Jerry. I'd forgotten about him. But he—

"What on earth!" Danesh held me out at arm's length. "What happened to you?"

That wasn't quite the reaction I'd been imagining. But I followed his gaze and glanced down at myself. My dress and skin were streaked with mud. I had already managed to transfer some to Danesh's shirt.

I could feel the heat of his hands on my arms, and for some reason that started me shivering. I spoke through chattering teeth. "I went—the rim—saw lights. Men—in ruins. Drug deal. Got to call—police."

Danesh put his arm around me and led me toward the back room. "We've got to get you warm. Jerry, you'd better call the police and let them know there's a problem out here. We'll sort out the details in a minute."

He nodded, "Di-did they see you?"

I shook my head but was too tired and cold to explain further. Jerry reached for the phone. I was grateful they didn't demand the whole story first. We could explain once the police were on the way.

Danesh pushed me into the bathroom. "Try to get some of that mud off. I'll find dry clothes."

I huddled over the sink, trying to wash mud from my arms in the trickle of lukewarm water. I glanced in the mirror and saw someone I hardly recognized. My damp hair tangled around my face, mud streaked my cheeks, and my eyes looked huge. I stared for a moment and then started laughing.

Danesh came in behind me. "What?"

"Look at me," I gasped. "Date night! You can't take me anywhere."

"You're hysterical."

I nodded but pressed my lips together to hold in my giggles. In the movies they always slapped people who got hysterical. I didn't want to be slapped.

Danesh studied me, frowning, then stepped forward and pulled me close.

My giggles evaporated. A minute later, my shivers eased, too.

"Better now?" he whispered.

I nuzzled his neck. "Mmm. You'll get all wet and muddy."

"I'll survive." I ran my tongue along his collarbone and then nipped his neck.

His arms tightened, and he drew in a quick breath. "I'm not sure this is the time or place for that, darlin', but I appreciate the sentiment."

He backed up and handed me a bundle of clothing. "The running shorts are mine, and they're clean. The T-shirt is from the sales counter. The jacket is Jerry's. Get into them and then we'll wrap you in a blanket." He backed out of the bathroom.

I quickly peeled off my clothes and rubbed my body down with the hand towel. I was far from clean, but getting warm was more important. The running shorts had a built-in liner, so I took off my panties, which were damp and clinging. My bra was gritty with mud from my sandals, so I discarded that as well. My cold nipples showed through the T-shirt like little buttons, but I zipped up Jerry's jacket to hide that sight. The jacket hung nearly to my knees, and I had to push up the sleeves to free my hands.

I stepped out of the bathroom barefoot. Danesh wrapped a blanket around me, hustled me to the sofa, and brought me a cup of hot coffee. I closed my hands around the warm mug and sipped.

Danesh sat beside me. "Give me your feet." He slid athletic socks on for me and then tucked the blanket around my feet. "Think you can explain now?"

I nodded but took another sip of coffee and kept my face close to the mug, feeling the heat. The adrenaline had worn off, and I wanted to curl up and sleep. But it wasn't over yet.

I settled back against the sofa with a sigh. Where to start? "You know the guy I was supposed to have a date with tonight?"

Danesh nodded, frowning.

"Turns out he was trying to get me out of the way. I found him in Falling House, giving a briefcase full of money to two other guys."

He stared, as if trying to process the information or maybe trying to decide if I was hallucinating. "What did you do?"

"I hid and they went past. But they took the board they'd used as a bridge, so I had to climb down into the canyon and back out again."

"You climbed down into the canyon. In a dress—" He blew out a breath. "You're sure they didn't see you?" He spoke calmly enough, but the fierce expression on his face reminded me again of an ancient warrior.

I shrugged. "If they had, I imagine they would have done something about it already."

Danesh jumped up, paced across the room, and came back. He squatted in front of me, his hands on my knees. "You could have been hurt. Or—worse."

I yawned, too tired to raise a hand to cover my mouth. "I'm all right."

He rubbed my legs through the blanket. "Warm enough now?"

I nodded, gazing into his eyes, hardly aware of the question. He might be bossy sometimes, but he had a nurturing streak a mile wide. I liked that. I liked his brown eyes, too, and the high cheekbones and the way he could look fierce but you could see the tenderness underneath, once you knew where to look.

Movement caught my attention, and I glanced toward the doorway to see Jerry. Danesh looked back at him too. "Are they on their way?"

Jerry nodded.

Danesh rose and pushed a hand through his hair. "All right. We should call back and explain. Can you describe the vehicle?"

"Dark green SUV. But I think there's a second one I didn't see. I don't think they came together."

"Okay, I'll call. They'll want a statement, so you might have to go to town. I could run over to your campsite and get you some more clothes and some shoes."

"It's—" I yawned. "All right." Maybe I should have worried about dealing with the police with bare legs and borrowed clothes, but so long as I could stay curled up in the blanket, I didn't much care. I finished the hot coffee and felt the warmth seeping from my stomach to my limbs. I forced myself to lean toward the table with the mug, instead of letting it fall from my hands.

As I put the cup down I noticed Danesh and Jerry both standing still, looking toward the doorway. Then I heard the growl and crunch of a car pulling in.

"That was fast," I said.

Danesh gave a noncommittal grunt. "Very fast. Stay here." He went to the front room, pulling the door closed behind him.

I heard the sound of another door opening. Then Danesh's voice, faint but audible. "We're closed for the night. I'm the only one here, and I'm on my way out."

I looked at Jerry, who stared back at me. The door between the rooms opened, and Danesh backed through it. Three men followed.

Two of them had guns. The third was Sean.

Twenty-Two

Sean glared at me. "I wish you'd stayed at my place."

I swallowed hard. "I wish I'd never gone there."

I clutched the blanket tighter around me as if it offered some kind of protection. The strangers blocked the doorway. One had reddish hair and wore a leather jacket. He was lean and haggard, as if he'd lived too hard for too long, like a battle-scarred rooster. The other was younger, with black hair and dark eyes that scanned the room before settling on me. His wide mouth stretched in a slow smile that had me pressing back into the couch.

Danesh edged between me and the men. Jerry had pressed back against the wall, staring like a rabbit in headlights.

Sean paced. "So what are we going to do about this?"

"Not much you can do," Danesh said. "Tie us up and get away."

My heart pounded in my ears. They hadn't seen me earlier—they couldn't have, or they would have stopped me before I ever got to the visitors center. So why were they here? I had the feeling I was missing some vital piece of information, but I couldn't think. I felt flushed now, almost too hot, but I hugged the blanket tight, trembling.

Sean looked at Danesh, at me, at Jerry. He spoke over his shoulder to the other men. "What do you think, guys? How should we take care of them?"

The dark one gave a short laugh. The redhead said, "You're the one who must take care of them.

We came to see that you do the job right."

The other man muttered, "That's right! We're not cleaning up your mess."

Sweat prickled my face even as I shivered. I'd been mistaken about Sean, but he couldn't be a killer. Could he?

Sean kept pacing. I leaned over to see around Danesh. I appreciated his desire to protect me, but I needed to know what was happening. And I knew using his body as a shield would only last as long as it took a bullet to cross the room.

"This is my life, you know!" Sean said. "I have an apartment, friends, a nice, easy job that keeps people from asking too many questions. This took years to set up." He stopped to glare at me. "I can't walk away from it all and start over."

The red-haired man said, "So do what you must do. Enough of your games."

The man held out his gun. "Prove you are man enough for this."

Sean glared at him. He reached for the gun. I saw Danesh bend his knees as if getting ready to spring.

Jerry cried out and pushed away from the wall, an arm outstretched.

Danesh shoved Sean into the red-haired man. They stumbled against the wall, and Sean went down on one knee.

The dark-haired man was grappling with Jerry. Danesh grabbed the door and swung it so it slammed against the criminal's back. He yelled, "Kylie, run!"

I tried to jump up but my legs tangled in the blanket. I struggled free and stumbled into the center of the room. Danesh was trying to wrestle the gun away from the red-haired man. Sean was on his feet. He turned toward me.

Someone must have bumped the light switch. The room went dark.

A gun went off. I screamed.

In the light spilling in from the front room, I saw Sean duck and glance back at the wrestling men. I willed my rubbery legs to move and raced through the door.

I banged the corner of the counter, bounced off, and careened through the front room.

Sean yelled something. I glanced back as I fumbled with the door handle. Sean was only a few steps behind me. I stumbled through the door and ran across the parking lot.

The night seemed pitch black after the lights of the visitors center. I heard a shout behind me but kept running. My breath choked on a sob. How long could Danesh and Jerry keep fighting? They might already be dead.

I had to get help. I had to hide.

I could only keep running.

My feet pounded the ground. I landed on a sharp rock and cried out in pain. I limped through the next step but kept moving. My heart hammered and my breath rasped, but instinct screamed through me: *Run, run!*

My foot slid in the mud. The socks were half hanging off my feet. I stumbled, caught myself, and ran on.

A shred of sane thought wrestled with the terror. I couldn't keep running blindly. I held my hands out in front of myself so I wouldn't crash into a tree, but I needed to get my bearings, figure out where I was. I needed to get away from Sean and make a plan.

But he must be right behind me! I couldn't stop, couldn't even risk slowing down or looking back.

Something sharp caught me across the shin. I yelped and stumbled forward as the pain burned like a hot knife.

I almost went down on my knees, but I managed to thrust a foot out in front of me.

The foot found no place to land. I pitched forward with a sickening lurch that left my stomach behind.

And then I was hurtling through the darkness, down into the canyon.

Twenty-Three

I hit something, bounced, scraped, and finally landed with a thud that rattled my whole body.

I lay in the dark, blinded, my head ringing, pain washing over me in great waves. My lungs screamed for air, but it seemed like I'd forgotten how to breathe.

Finally I dragged in a breath. I closed my eyes and focused on breathing, waiting for the world to settle into place.

Rain misted my face, so I must be lying on my back. My head felt heavier than my feet. I shifted and realized I was lying on a slope with my head pointing down.

I tried to concentrate on those little details. I couldn't handle anything more. Panic fluttered around me, but I refused to think about anything but the present moment.

I flexed my fingers. When that worked, I moved my hands over my body, up to my face. My head throbbed, but when I felt around my skull, I didn't find any serious damage.

I had to move. The thought battered at the back of my mind, a panicky whisper that I tried to ignore. I had to run. Hide. He was after me. I had to get away.

I clenched my teeth hard, as if I could bite back the pain and fear. Memories crowded in, like panicked ghosts wailing at the edges of my mind. Guns, strange men. Dangerous, threatening men. Danesh trying to protect me, the gun going off. My own helpless, panicked flight. Helpless. Worthless. Unable to fight, unable even to scream.

I tried to focus on this one moment, the physical sensations of my aching body as I lay on the hard, damp ground. The cold against my bare calves, the lump of rock pressing into my shoulder. That focus helped keep me grounded in the present. Never mind that this present wasn't a place I wanted to be. I had to deal with reality. But I didn't have to also deal with nightmares. Not now.

The little whimpers in my throat faded to short gasping breaths. I held on to this moment, this single slice of reality. Now to move forward. I didn't have to like it, but I had to do it. One step at a time.

I tried bending my knees, and that seemed to work. So far, so good. But the cold seeped through my thin jacket and I started to shiver.

Ignore that. I needed to get my feet below my head before I could stand up. I tried to move but only twitched, my body not sure yet how to give the right signals. Finally I rolled onto my right side, bringing my knees up toward my chest. I slid a little and wound up huddled face down, my head in my hands. Nausea swamped me and I tried not to retch. My head felt far too large. I swallowed hard and breathed, breathed, breathed, until my head settled back down to size.

I wanted to stay there, ignore the world, sleep until all the pain and fear went away. But somewhere above me, Sean was looking for me. Had he seen me fall or guessed what had happened? Did he think I was dead? I couldn't trust that he would leave without making sure.

When I was fairly certain I wouldn't throw up, I pushed myself slowly to my knees. The world swung around me. Bile rose in my throat. I closed my eyes and listened to the night but heard only the wind.

The world settled into place, and the nausea faded again. I had to move. Sean was out there, after me. I didn't know what had happened to Danesh or Jerry. I needed to get help, needed to go back and help my friends, needed to do *something*. Tears joined the rain on my cheeks.

I covered my face with my hands. I couldn't do anything in this state. The panic was too close, threatening to devour me. I needed to get somewhere safe where I could think, find my balance, make plans. Be safe.

I looked around, searching for inspiration. My eyes seemed to be adjusting to the dark, so at least I could tell the difference between ground and sky. I squinted up toward the rim. I hadn't fallen that far, fifteen or twenty feet. Maybe I could get back up. But then what?

A beam of light sliced across the black sky directly above me. I whimpered and tucked my head down, hoping the light wouldn't pick me out. At least the jacket was dark and, by now, muddy. I lay still for seconds that felt like hours. My skin chilled and my feet went numb. I thought I heard faint scuffling sounds on the rim above, and then nothing more.

I cautiously peered up toward the canyon rim and saw nothing.

I needed to get out of there. I could move. I had to. I pushed against the ground and staggered to my feet.

Pain screamed through my left ankle and it threatened to collapse. I couldn't hold back a cry.

I tested the ankle gingerly and discovered I could put some weight on it, but the pain brought tears to my eyes. It probably wasn't broken, but definitely sprained. My shin throbbed, too, around a burning spot where I'd felt the flash of pain earlier, before I fell. I'd probably cut myself on something, might even be bleeding. I couldn't do anything about the pain but ignore it.

I shivered as cold air rushed past me. Where could I go? I didn't dare climb back to the rim path until I was sure Sean was gone. But without getting up to the rim, I couldn't reach the campground, my car, a phone, anything. I could hike across the canyon to the trail on the other side, but that meant two or three miles of walking before I could get back to the campground. I didn't think I could do it. I gave a hiccoughing sob.

The clouds shifted, and moonlight spilled across the canyon. For a moment the smooth lines of a tower seemed to glow above me, like an offering.

The Castle. An eight-hundred-year-old fortress, if the archaeologists' guesses were right. It was still a sturdy defense, with walls twenty feet high. It perched on the canyon rim with its one doorway opening into the canyon. You couldn't reach that doorway from the rim, because the walls were built all the way to the edge. You could only reach the doorway from down in the canyon—by climbing up a "ladder" of notches in the rocks.

But this ladder had an advantage over the one I'd tried to climb down at Stronghold House. At the Castle, early archaeologists had bolted a chain into the rock to aid their access, and it still hung alongside the ladder. If I could get up the cliff and inside the Castle, no one could reach me unless they climbed up after me. And if they did that, I'd be above them, able to kick or hit while they were busy holding on.

It was a crazy idea. What good would it do to hide in the Castle?

I heard a shout and a clatter, like falling rocks. My heart jumped and I bolted.

I didn't think about where I was going. I just ran. I headed for the Castle because it was in front of me, because I'd been thinking how safe it seemed. I was working on fear, not logic.

My ankle throbbed with each step. Prickly bushes scraped my calves. My feet slid in the mud. When I reached the base of the cliffs below the ruin, I pressed close to the wall and felt for the chain. I closed my hand around the ice-cold metal.

I looked up at the canyon rim. Sean's flashlight bobbed along the path, the beam swinging across the trees on the rim. He was headed away, toward the campground. He hadn't yet figured out I was down in the canyon. In a minute I could be in the Castle. I could be safe.

I pulled the wet socks tight over my feet, wiped my hands on Jerry's jacket, and pushed the hair out of my eyes. Then I grabbed the chain and leaned back on it. I found a notch for my good foot and stepped my weight up onto it. I reached a hand higher and heaved my body up. I whimpered as I put weight on my twisted ankle and decided to use my knee instead. The knee throbbed as I pressed it into the hard rock, but a few seconds later I had my other foot back on the wall.

I could do this. I could escape.

I dragged myself up the cliff, refusing to look either up or down. I told myself that if I could reach the Castle, I would be safe. I wouldn't think otherwise or worry about the next step. I'd be protected. Hidden. That was all that mattered now. Safe. Safe.

My hands went numb on the cold chain. I no longer noticed rain on my face, and the wind moved through the canyon with a murmur rather than a roar. I heard the river below me, gurgling and splashing as it rushed over boulders and poured down the canyon. I refused to think about the deep canyon slipping away behind me. I was almost up the cliff.

Light flashed across my arms. I gasped and twitched. One foot started to slip, but I clung to the chain with trembling arms, fighting vertigo as my body swung.

A shout echoed across the canyon. The light moved away from me, and I glanced over my shoulder. Sean was striding along the canyon rim, using the flashlight to light his path. Then the beam came back to me, pinning me to the cliff. He had seen me.

I whimpered and reached for the next hold. My hand slid over the top of the rock. I clenched the chain with frozen fingers and moved trembling limbs higher. I got an arm over the cliff and wriggled forward, finally pulling up my legs. I ignored the hard, cold rock against my skin as I crawled through the little doorway on hands and knees.

I huddled inside, shaking, hugging my knees to my chest. The small room was black except for the paler dark of the doorway and the sky above, where the roof had collapsed. I heard voices, faint whispers carried by the wind. Sean and the gunmen making plans? Someone from the campground who had wandered over and asked a question? The police at last? No, I would have heard their cars.

Where were the police? What had happened back in the visitors center? Could Danesh be dead? I sobbed and buried my face in my knees. I'd only just found him. I couldn't lose him yet.

But what could I do?

I lifted my head and took a few shuddering breaths. I couldn't give up. I had to gain control of myself, I had to figure out what to do! I spent several torturous minutes wrestling with the panic. But this time I won.

I listened hard, hoping for a shout from a familiar voice, telling me it was safe to come out. But the only whispers came from the wind sliding past the ruined walls.

For one fleeting moment, I thought of Danesh tucking the blanket around my feet. But I didn't have time for such thoughts and the grief they would bring. Sean knew where I had gone.

What would he do? He could get to the Castle easily enough from the rim, but he couldn't get inside. From the canyon rim, he'd have to climb a twenty-foot wall or else knock it down. Could he do that? Maybe with his SUV. I shuddered at that thought, for myself and for the ancient ruin. But that would make noise and surely draw attention from the campground. And damage his car, maybe prevent his escape anyway. He wouldn't dare.

Some part of me still threatened to drift off into that shadowy dreamland of waiting, still, silent, and powerless, until someone else decided what happened next. I couldn't give in. I had to pay attention. I had to protect myself.

I would not beat myself up because I had panicked. I had made a mistake. I could learn from that and move on.

I simply had to keep showing up and doing the best I could.

The only way someone could reasonably get to me was through the doorway. My hideout was only safe if I protected the entrance. I crawled back to the three-foot-high doorway and peeked out. I was afraid someone might try to shoot me if I moved my head into view, but I had to get some idea of what they were doing. I kept low and searched for Sean's light.

I didn't see it, but a sound from below warned me of the choice Sean had made. I leaned out the doorway and looked down the cliff to be sure.

A dark form, with moonlight glinting off his hair, edged up the cliff like a lizard. He was coming after me.

Twenty-Four

I ducked back with a whimper. My first instinct was to scramble back inside the ruins and hide. But once I was trapped within those walls, I could do nothing but wait for Sean to find me.

I knelt, my hands pressed down against the stone as if I could draw power from the cliff itself. I had to act. I was in a position of strength. I had to use it. I would not be a victim this time.

Sean was only a few feet down, hauling himself up more quickly than I had done. I backed through the doorway and searched the ground for some loose object to use as a weapon. My hands closed on something; from the shape, I identified a block. I hesitated, the archaeologist in me protesting even now at disturbing an artifact. I swept my hand across the floor and found a loose rock the size of an orange.

I scurried back to the doorway and saw fingers creeping over the edge of the cliff, thick, pale worms searching for a hold. I whimpered and clutched the rock to my chest. Then with no more time for thought, I stretched forward and smashed the rock down on the fingers.

Sean howled and the fingers disappeared. I leaned forward to look over the edge.

He clung to the cliff, one arm wrapped around the chain and the other hand held close to his chest. He looked up at me. "You didn't need to do that. I'm not going to hurt you."

"Then why don't you go away?" I said, my voice high and shaky.

"Let me come up and we can talk."

"I don't have anything to say to you." I dragged air through my tight throat. My hands gripped the rock, my fingers chilled and stiff, rough ridges digging into my palms. The sensations kept me here, grounded, focused. When I spoke again, my voice sounded almost calm.

"Take your money and go home to your fancy apartment and say goodbye to it, because you'll never live there again. The best thing you can do is run. You should have listened to Danesh." My voice broke on his name and my voice wavered as I choked out, "And if you hurt him, I'll kill you myself!"

He gazed up at me and actually smiled. "You wouldn't. You're not the type."

"You don't know anything about my type."

His free hand moved back to the chain. "I know there's something between us. Don't you see, I was trying to protect you by keeping you away tonight. Because I care. I'm sure we can work something out—think of all the things we could do with this money."

Leave it to a man to think one kiss meant you were his slave forever. He slid his hand up the chain.

"Forget it," I said. "And if your fingers touch this cliff again, I'll smash them even harder."

His smile faded and his hand retreated. "You don't want me, fine. But the money—"

"It's not all about money." I noticed his hand moving down toward his pocket.

The hand came out with a gun.

My body jerked but I resisted the instinct to jump back. He raised the gun. I threw the rock at his hand.

It hit him in the chin. He didn't utter a sound, but I heard the thunk of the rock hitting him. I watch him slide down the cliff, hit the slope twenty feet below, and topple backward. A bush crackled as he rolled through it. His body tumbled and slid down into the canyon. The moon must have come out, because I could see all the way down to the river that rushed past fifty feet below. Sean splashed into the water and sank. He popped up fifteen feet farther downstream and then disappeared.

I huddled back against the wall, shaking with sobs. "I had to do it!" I gasped. "I had to!"

I closed my eyes, but I kept seeing him falling, the way he had seemed to bounce and roll before splashing into the river. Could he have survived that? I had been thinking only of stopping him, not killing him.

My own words echoed back to me. "I'll kill you myself." I hadn't meant it literally. It was a figure of speech. Now Danesh might be dead, Jerry, too, because I had led criminals to them, and maybe I had killed Sean ...

I don't know how long I huddled there, but finally the shaking slowed to faint tremors. I knew I had no choice, that he would have killed me otherwise, but that didn't stop the cold that spread through my chest.

I turned my head and pressed my cheek against the block wall of the ruins. I had come to study ancient people, gone for centuries, to learn something about their lives and, in a sense, keep them alive in the modern world. Now I had most likely killed a man. It didn't make sense.

I wanted to crawl back inside the Castle and hide, willing reality to fade away. But as I tried to push the memory of Sean's falling body out of my mind, other thoughts rushed in to fill the space. Two dangerous men were still out there, waiting for Sean to return. Danesh and Jerry might still be alive. If they were, for how long?

I had to do something. But what?

I pressed my hands to my face. One step at a time. Before I could help anyone else, I had to get out of the ruin. My safe haven, which had seemed such a great place to get *to* when I was on the run, was not so great to get *from*. I'd have to go back down the way I'd come up.

I shuddered at the thought and closed my eyes to block out the yawning depths of the canyon. I couldn't do it. Not after what I'd seen. I'd wait where I was. Surely the other men would leave soon if Sean didn't come back. They weren't local, and I didn't even know their names—they didn't have as much to lose by leaving witnesses. The police would come—they must be nearly here. It seemed like hours had passed since Jerry had called them.

Something nagged at me, something I needed to remember, to understand. I pressed my hands over my closed eyes. I had to think back over the night. I didn't want to remember, but I was sure I had missed some important clue with everything happening so fast.

I had overheard the men and hidden. I had made it to the visitors center. Jerry had called the police, but only a few minutes later those men had shown up. Why had they come back?

And then I knew. Jerry had not called the police. He must have called Sean. How else had Sean known to come to the visitors center? And the men had walked in like they knew the situation, with no questions.

It was impossible. Jerry, one of them? No way. And yet nothing else made sense. Sean hadn't gone far, and Jerry had called him back. Why, I couldn't fathom. But it had to be true.

My thoughts grudgingly took the next step. What about Danesh? Was he involved?

I ignored my first instinctive protest and forced myself to consider the question seriously. Danesh had been with me while Jerry called. But then he'd been out of my sight for a few minutes, getting me clothing. Had they discussed what to do about me?

I shook my head. If they were both involved, why call Sean at all? They could have gotten rid of me in so many other ways, ways that looked more like an accident. Or even delayed, pretended the phone was out, bought some time for the men to escape. And why start the fight so I could run? If that was part of a plan for dealing with me, it was too elaborate to make sense. Besides, if Danesh had known something was happening that night, he could have easily kept me away or insisted on taking me to my campsite.

I remembered Jerry pushing away from the wall with a cry, reaching out. I'd assumed he was joining the fight. Had he really been trying to stop Danesh from doing anything? Or had he finally realized how far in he'd gotten himself and started to have regrets? I couldn't know, and it was safer to assume the worst.

I sighed. I wasn't certain I understood anything. I believed Danesh was on my side, which helped make up for the pain of Jerry's betrayal. And Danesh's interest in me was honest, unlike Sean's.

But what if Danesh was already dead? My chest felt tight, and I hugged myself, struggling against tears. He couldn't be dead. I couldn't bear that.

I tipped my head back and looked up at the night sky, drawing in raspy breaths. The moon, a day or two past full, shone down on me among wispy clouds. A few bright stars pricked through the haze of the sky. I felt the breeze on my face and smelled the earthy, spicy scent of wet desert. I was here, now. That was all I had to work with.

It felt like hours had passed since I'd fled the visitors center, but it was probably only a matter of minutes. I might still have time to do some good. Danesh might still be alive, and if so, he needed me. He didn't have anyone else right now.

I had to think logically. The drug runners had expected Sean to take care of us. Sean had run out after me, but at some point he had gotten one of the guns. Had he already killed Danesh—and possibly Jerry, for knowing too much?

Maybe the other men would have waited for Sean to find me before they did anything else. If Sean couldn't find me, it would be better to run from drug charges than run from murder charges. And maybe Danesh had escaped during the fight anyway. Maybe he had already gone for help.

My heart leapt at the thought—not only because it would mean Danesh was still alive, but because then I could wait for rescue. I immediately felt guilty for the thought, but I'd never asked to be a hero. I'd never waited for a strong man to rescue me—and had certainly never had that experience before—but I'd take it now.

I shook my head. I couldn't count on rescue. If Danesh was still in trouble, I needed to do something right away. I couldn't predict what the other men would do if Sean didn't come back. I couldn't take chances.

Could I possibly work my way around the Castle instead of going back down the cliff? Maybe it wasn't as hard as it looked. No, the ledge was only a few inches wide, with a rounded, unstable edge and nothing to grip on the block walls. The cliff down was the only way out.

I leaned forward to look over the edge. The image of Sean falling filled my mind, and I pulled back, sick and dizzy.

That was the past. I had to focus on now. I took a deep breath and turned around. I held on to the top of the chain and started to lower my feet over the edge. I would not look down again. I wouldn't think about falling or worry about what I could do after I got down. I would focus on my hands on the chain, my feet on the rock, moving one step at a time.

My feet were so numb that I could hardly feel the rock. At least the cold numbed the pain in my ankle, too. I watched my hands on the chain, feeling almost as if they were someone else's hands. They responded to my commands, but they didn't quite seem connected to me. Was this hypothermia or shock or my mind trying to retreat from reality?

It didn't matter. I had to keep moving. Left hand down. Right hand down. Left foot down. Right foot down.

My foot hit solid ground so suddenly that it threw me off balance. I wobbled, clutching the chain with both hands until my mind finally registered that I could let go now. I paused to find my balance and then hobbled along the path that led up to the rim.

By the time I made it to the rim trail, my body seemed to be working better, warmed slightly by the exertion. I peered over the edge cautiously, half expecting to see a gun pointing at me. Nothing. I took the last few steps to the rim trail and stood on wobbly legs.

A dark shape swooped overhead. I gasped and cringed, but it was only an owl, hunting on silent wings.

I still hadn't consciously decided on the next step, but I found myself moving toward the visitors center. The glow of its window flickered through the trees, calling me. Was anyone still inside? Was anyone alive?

When I turned at the parking lot, I saw Sean's SUV and a battered Land Rover I didn't recognize, which the other men had probably come in. It would be a good way to get through the desert from a secret landing site.

I stared at the visitors center. What could I do? Two men—three if Jerry was still on their side—and at least one gun. If Danesh was still alive, he was probably tied up or hurt. I couldn't count on any help from him. Whatever I did, I had to assume I'd be doing it alone.

Everything was up to me. And I was aching, exhausted, and out of ideas.

Twenty-Five

I kept to the edge of the parking lot as I moved toward the building. When I reached Danesh's truck, I paused with my hand on it. My eyes stung as I remembered a drive that now seemed long ago. Then a thought worked its way into my foggy mind. My backpack!

I moved to the driver's side door, keeping the truck between me and the building. I grabbed the door handle and had barely enough sense to pause. I didn't want to attract attention with noise. Or light. Did his interior light come on automatically when the door opened? I closed my eyes and thought back. Yes, I was pretty sure it did.

I rested my forehead on the cool window. Why couldn't anything be simple? I peeked at the visitors center. The window glowed on the side wall, but that wouldn't have a view of the front parking lot. They could only see me if they opened the door. I decided it was worth the chance.

I took a deep breath, staring through the truck's windows at the visitors center door.

The door opened.

The dark-haired man stood silhouetted in the open doorway. "No sign of him. What is he doing?"

I froze, praying that the man wouldn't be able to see me in the dark. The truck blocked his view of me, unless he happened to look at the passenger side window and could see all the way through the cab to my face on the other side.

I told myself moving would only attract attention. I told myself the light spilling out the doorway would glint off the passenger window and help hide me.

I willed the man to go back inside.

He turned his head and called over his shoulder. "He's not coming back! He's run off."

The other man's voice barely reached me. "We've got his money. He'll be back."

The younger thug stepped outside and stared into the darkness. I held my breath.

He shook his head and turned back. "We should finish this ourselves and get out of here." The door closed behind him.

My legs went weak, and I sagged against the truck door. Close. Too close. But I was fine. He hadn't seen me, I was okay.

His last comment suggested they hadn't yet killed anyone, but I didn't have much time. I needed to get to my phone and pray that I could reach someone.

I grabbed the door handle, held my breath, and pulled open the door. It sounded loud to me, but surely they wouldn't notice from inside. I slipped into the cab and snapped off the overhead light. I left the door partly open, to avoid the sound of its closing.

I leaned across the seat and fumbled in my backpack on the floor. I found my phone. It had power! And reception! Barely, but one bar flickered on and off. I dialed a number that was starting to be too familiar.

The explanation seemed to take forever. We could barely hear each other and I didn't dare raise my voice. Finally I got across the bare facts, and they said the police would come. But it would take twenty or thirty minutes. They wanted me to stay on the line, but when the connection failed I didn't bother trying to call back.

I lay across the seat, cold and exhausted. But I couldn't rest. I didn't know if we could afford to wait twenty or thirty minutes. The men inside sounded impatient. Where could I go for help?

I could try the campground, but I'd have to hike

the half-mile on my bad ankle, wake people, and explain. Robert might still be out with Lily, and the other tourists from two nights before had probably moved on, so I'd have to convince strangers to believe me and take action.

Then we'd have to get back here. That would take as long as waiting for the police and put other people in danger. Our little community had done a great job with one unarmed man, but two armed criminals? I couldn't drag more innocent people into this.

A single shiver shook me. I wasn't shivering nearly enough. I dug into my backpack again and changed into dry socks and tennis shoes. At least it gave me something to do. I shrugged out of the oversized jacket, put on the thin sweater I'd brought in case the evening got cool—ha, ha—and put the jacket back on for an extra layer.

That done, I had to face the question of what to do next. If I didn't do anything, they might yet decide to kill Danesh and Jerry. If I did the wrong thing, I could make matters worse. I was relatively safe now, and that was something. I wouldn't help anyone by giving the gunmen another hostage or another victim. But I couldn't wait and do nothing while they murdered my friends.

I stared at the visitors center. I had to come up with a plan! I needed a weapon—my pepper spray! It shot almost ten feet. I could knock on the door—they'd think it was Sean—and then squirt the man who answered. It would only take care of one of them, temporarily ... I'd have to watch which way his gun was aiming ... It was the start of a plan.

I dug into the outside pocket of my backpack. My wallet was there, but no pepper spray. I checked the other outside pocket and then the main bag, just in case. Nothing. Had Sean somehow taken it? When?

I checked every pocket again. Nope. It was gone.

I squeezed my eyes tightly closed and pressed my lips together. I didn't have the pepper spray. I had to let go of the idea. Move on.

I took a deep breath and opened my eyes. Okay, so no pepper spray.

Maybe I could find some kind of weapon or tool in one of the vehicles. A tire iron, something like that. I found a first aid kit and some bungee cords behind the seat, and then noticed the large, built-in box in the truck bed. That must be where Danesh kept his tools. I stepped outside to look at it—padlocked, of course.

I looked at Jerry's car, Sean's SUV, and the Land Rover. The thought of creeping around the parking lot, in full view if anyone opened the door again, was enough to have me drawing back into the shadows. And I'd have to deal with door noises and interior lights, assuming the vehicles were even unlocked.

I glanced at the building. Then I noticed the small shed along the side, by the garden, and remembered Danesh's comment, "We keep the good weapons in the shed." They'd have tools in there! Rakes and hoes and shovels. I could use a good shovel. And I'd be away from the front door while I searched.

I ran for the side of the building, ducking under the window to pass it. I reached the shed and grabbed the door handle. Then I noticed the padlock.

I stared for half a minute, not wanting to believe. I pulled on it. I leaned my weight on the door. No good.

I obviously was not cut out for rescue work. I did better digging in the dirt and pondering ancient dead people. I should forget the whole thing and wait for the police.

But what about Danesh? How much longer would the men wait before deciding to take care of the remaining prisoners themselves and make their escape? So far I hadn't heard a gunshot. One might come at any moment, and then I'd know I had wasted too much time. I shivered. Even if the police arrived quickly, the drug runners would surely hear the vehicles, and then we'd have a hostage situation. I had to do something. But what? What?

I wanted to scream and pound on the shed door. I wanted to kick at the walls. I wanted to throw something.

An idea popped into my head.

I turned and surveyed the garden, remembering the line of display squash topping the fence poles.

My shoes squished and slipped in the mud as I fumbled in the dark until I found the squash. I pulled a few off the poles. They were dried out and barely had any weight. I huffed in annoyance but refused to give up my idea now.

I chose a squash about the size of a softball and felt for the hole in the bottom, where the post had poked into it. I crouched and scooped mud into the hole, keeping one eye on the building. I filled two more, one as backup. Okay. One step down. I paused to think through my idea. I knew my tired brain was working slowly, so I needed to think more carefully. I couldn't let the need to hurry cause me to make mistakes.

I made a sort of bag from my jacket front and piled in a few more light squash. I glanced around the garden, wondering if I'd missed anything useful. The fence poles were wired into the chicken wire; it would take too long to pry one loose.

Some of the plants were strung up on sticks. One stick seemed taller and thicker than the rest. I pulled it out of the ground. It appeared to be the handle broken off of a shovel or hoe. I would have preferred the handle with a nice heavy shovel blade on the end, but this was better than nothing. I supported my jacket-front full of squash with one hand, grabbed the stick with my free hand, and scurried out of the garden.

I moved toward the front of the visitors center, pausing when I was in line with the front wall but about ten feet from the corner. I could see the door, but if anyone came out I could duck back out of sight.

I bit my lip and tried to put a plan together. If I could separate the men and take them by surprise, I might—just might—have a chance at stopping them. My plan depended on a lot of variables, too many for my liking. Would Danesh be able to lend a hand? Which side would Jerry choose now? Would the drug runners behave the way I wanted them to or do something totally unexpected? Given my recent luck, I didn't want to answer that question.

My breathing came fast, and I felt lightheaded. Little trembles shook me. I had to grab control before panic swamped me and I fainted or did something stupid.

I forced myself to breathe deeply and slowly. I focused on the feel of the cold night air on my face, the hair matted to one cheek, my aching legs and back and throbbing ankle. I shoved aside any emotion over being cold and tired, weak and injured, and focused on the sensations. I smelled damp earth and growing things. I heard the whisper of rustling trees.

I was here, in this moment. From here I could step forward. I couldn't let myself worry about the future. Only this moment and the next step mattered.

I took a deep breath and whispered, "I have to try. For Danesh."

I glanced around and identified my escape route, if things should go wrong. I could get into the trees quickly and hopefully lose anyone following.

Time to move. I stood the shovel handle in the mud so I had a hand free. The building was built of cinder blocks with a corrugated tin roof. I nodded to myself. I took one of the small, dried-out squash and lobbed it onto the roof. It hit the tin with a bang and rattled as it rolled all the way down. I jumped even though I'd expected the sound.

I hefted the mud-filled squash and waited. Moments later, the door opened and Red Hair rushed out. My body jerked, but I fought instinct and stayed in place. The man turned to look up at the roof. He held a gun.

I wound up my swing. He glanced my way and

the gun moved toward me. I stepped forward and released.

The squash slammed into his face, right between the eyes. He toppled backward and collapsed on the pavement.

I grabbed the next weighted squash and eyed the door, but no one else came out. I grabbed the wooden handle like a bat and crept toward the fallen man, darting glances at the door. He made a choking sound and twitched. I saw the gun by his hand and picked it up, letting the squashes fall so I had a hand for the shovel handle and one for the gun.

The man's breathing settled into a regular if raspy rhythm, but he didn't move. I backed away, trying to decide on the next step. If the other man came to the doorway now, he'd see his fallen friend and that would put him on guard. I might not have a second chance at a pitch like that and couldn't assume I'd succeed again.

I had the gun, but I wasn't sure how to use it, and the thought of shooting someone made me sick. I might have already killed Sean. I didn't want to leave a trail of bodies behind me this night. Maybe I could shoot him in the leg. But that would take aim, and I could hardly hold the gun steady. Plus, what if it had a safety I had to unhook or something? I didn't think Red Hair would wait while I messed around.

I forced my body to move toward the door. Surely the other man would come to investigate any moment. I had to take care of him before the first one recovered.

Then I finally noticed the sounds from inside. Grunts and thuds that suggested a struggle.

I stood with the shovel handle and gun, trying to think. Then I ran through the door, slammed it behind me, and locked it. At least one man was out of the fight for now.

In the back room, two figures wrestled. Danesh's hair tumbled loose from his ponytail and tangled in his face. The crook landed a blow to his stomach. Danesh grabbed him in a bear hug and they stumbled out of my line of sight. I didn't see Jerry.

I raised the gun, but I couldn't shoot without the chance of hitting Danesh, if I could get the gun to work at all.

Maybe I should let Danesh finish the battle. He seemed to be winning, now that he had a hand around the guy's throat. But what if he didn't?

Too much thinking. I shoved the gun in my jacket pocket and hefted the stick. I stepped through the doorway to the back room, squeezed the wooden handle tighter in trembling fingers, and swung the weapon low as the pair staggered toward me. It caught my target across the back of both knees. He folded backward with a grunt, pulling Danesh down on top of him. I heard a crack, maybe from a head hitting the floor.

I raised the stick but couldn't get a clear shot. Danesh rolled the guy onto his stomach and pinned his arms behind his back. Danesh tossed his hair out of his face and gasped for breath. "Other guy?"

"Down for now. I have his gun." I realized my hands stung from the force of swinging the stick. I dropped it. "Jerry?" I scanned the room and spotted a still form stretched out on the sofa. Jerry's shirt was open, and blood seeped through a white bandage over his shoulder.

I guess I cried out. Danesh said, "He's alive. Help me with this guy. There's some rope in that corner cabinet, bottom shelf." He gave me a quick smile. "Didn't tell them that, though."

The smuggler was struggling and cursing, but Danesh managed to keep him pinned down and dodge the flailing feet while I found the rope. I tied his hands, and then Danesh made a few quick moves I could hardly follow, and the man wound up hogtied, his hands and feet behind him, separated by about six inches of rope.

Danesh stood and blew out a breath. "Now what were you saying about the other guys?"

"I hit him with a squash. I knocked him out, but I don't know for how long." I fished the gun out of my pocket and offered it to Danesh. "He's in the parking lot. I locked the front door."

"A squash? Wait—which guy are we talking about?"

Right. For a moment I'd forgotten about Sean. "The guy who just came out. But I don't think we have to worry about Sean, either."

Danesh's eyebrows went up, but he just went past me to the front room, opened the door, and dragged Red Hair back inside. The man had his eyes halfway open, but he couldn't walk a straight line. When Danesh pushed him against the wall and told him to sit, he slid down the wall and sprawled in a heap. As Danesh tied him up he frowned at the man's bloody, muddy face. "Did you say you hit him with a *squash?*"

I nodded. "Filled with mud. It acted like a softball. I didn't mention that I sometimes pitch ..."

Danesh started to laugh. "Honey, I'm glad you're on my team."

Twenty-Six

The dark-haired man rolled onto his side. He wiggled and jerked but could only move a few inches across the floor. "We have half a million dollars—it's all yours, if you let us go."

"Forget it." Danesh turned toward the front room. "I'll call the police."

"I already called," I said. "My phone was still in your car."

Danesh swung back toward me and lifted me off the floor in a hug. "I could get used to having you around."

I felt my face heating and smiled back. "They're supposed to be on their way, but I'm not sure how much they understood."

"I'll call back." Danesh glanced at Jerry. "I'd better make sure they're sending an ambulance." He went to the front room to call.

I ignored the man who was still pleading and bargaining and went to stand over Jerry. He looked gray, but his chest still rose and fell, his breath raspy. How had he gotten into this? How would he get himself out? Or had I been wrong, and he was another innocent bystander?

Danesh came up and put his arm around me. We both gazed down at Jerry.

Finally I said, "What happened?"

"He was shot during that first struggle, when you escaped. They let me patch him up. You saved our lives, you know."

"Me? I ran."

"That's what did it. After the other guy—Sean?—

went after you, they talked about killing us, but decided having one witness and two dead bodies was worse than having three witnesses and no murders, so they waited."

The man on the floor said, "We're not killers! We let you save him, right? We never planned to kill you, just scare you, come on, man—"

Danesh glanced back, and his lip curled in disgust. "I'm sure they didn't intend to leave anyone alive, but they seemed determined to make Sean do the dirty work. Maybe trying to avoid murder charges if they did get caught, or maybe as some kind of test for Sean or because he screwed up. I gather they haven't been working together long, and these two don't think much of Sean, but they wanted him in so deep he couldn't back out."

I tried to tune out the ranting behind us and focus on Jerry. "How badly do you think he's hurt?"

"I don't know. I don't think the bullet hit any organs, but I'm not a doctor."

"So he got shot when I escaped. Thanks for that, by the way." I hesitated, but decided to plunge on. "I wondered if he was … if he could be …"

"I know." Danesh sighed. "He had to be working with them. That's the only way this makes sense." His eyes looked shiny, and I was glad I hadn't had to break the news.

The man spoke behind us. "Your friend knew, he was smart. We can cut you in the same way—"

Danesh whirled on him. "We're not interested in your deals!" He glanced around the room, took two steps to the counter with the coffee maker, and tore a couple of paper towels off a roll. He stuffed them in the man's mouth as a gag.

Danesh rose, looking fierce. He frowned down at Jerry and shook his head. "I keep wondering why. I'm sure he didn't do drugs. We don't make much money, and he wasn't really happy here, but still …"

"I saw how people treated him," I said. "It must have grated over time, but it still doesn't seem like a reason to turn to crime."

Danesh rubbed his eyes. "During the fight, he was helping me, I'm sure of it. I don't think I would have survived if Jerry hadn't jumped in. They must've had some kind of hold over him, but I can't believe he would let them hurt either one of us. I'm sure he was fighting on our side when it came time to choose."

I nodded, hoping Danesh was right.

He took my arms and looked into my eyes. "Could we ... not say anything to the police yet about Jerry? When he wakes up, we can ask him about it and decide then. But if he doesn't make it, there's no reason to drag his name through the mud, hurt his parents, Maureen ..."

I would have agreed to nearly anything to ease the pain in his face. "All right. I don't know anything for sure, anyway, so I can keep my guesses to myself."

"Thanks." The slightest smile touched his lips, and I wondered when I would see a real smile again. He pulled me into a hug. "You haven't told me yet what happened to Sean. Are you sure we shouldn't be worried about him?"

I felt myself start to tremble. Danesh's grip tightened. "Kylie. What happened out there?"

"I think he's dead." My words came out in short gasps. "I hit him with a rock. He fell—fell down to the river. From the cliff. I killed him."

Danesh snuggled me close. "It's all right," he whispered. "Everything will be all right." He held me as I clung to him and sobbed into his shoulder.

My trembling slowed and my sobs faded to shaky breaths. The warmth from Danesh's skin seeped into me, banishing the last of my chill. I sighed and nestled my cheek against his shoulder. I felt safe and comfortable there—more safe and comfortable than I'd felt in a long time, despite the night's trauma. I didn't want to let go. Ever.

Danesh brushed kisses across my temple. Then he lifted his head and turned his face toward the door. I heard the sound of sirens drawing closer.

"I hope one of those is the ambulance," Danesh said.

Red Hair mumbled something and squirmed. The other man spit out the sodden wad of paper towels. "It's Sean's fault! We got dragged into this, too. Help us, and we'll—"

Danesh and I ignored him and went out to meet the police.

Twenty-Seven

Once the police understood the situation, things moved quickly. A helicopter took Jerry to the hospital, and an EMT bandaged my ankle and checked my other cuts and bruises. A search team came out to find Sean. The police took the other criminals into town, and Danesh and I followed in his truck. I dozed on the way, and even the police station coffee couldn't fully wake me up again.

I made it through questioning, constantly reminding myself to state only what happened and not what I guessed or assumed. If I sometimes had to pause before answering, surely my exhaustion was enough of an excuse. If the police were any good at their job, they would suspect Jerry anyway, but that wasn't my problem.

My breath hitched when I described knocking Sean off the cliff, but the police didn't seem concerned about what I'd done. They said it was clearly self-defense. I didn't think that would stop the nightmares, but at least I didn't have to worry about legal repercussions.

Finally they let Danesh and me leave. By that point, I couldn't even walk a straight line to his truck. He helped boost me in and I sank back against the seat with my eyes closed.

It felt like only a couple of minutes passed before the truck stopped. I opened my eyes. Maybe only a couple of minutes had passed—we were still in town.

"My place," Danesh said. "We can get you a hotel room if you'd prefer, but I thought this would be easier."

I hadn't really thought about where we were going, but I wasn't anxious to drive all the way back to my campsite and sleep on the ground. And finding a hotel would take time and effort, too. My voice sounded hoarse when I spoke. "Can I assume you're too exhausted to take advantage of me?"

He chuckled. "I like to think I'm too honorable, but either way, I promise not to take advantage of you."

"Too bad." I yawned and stretched, then practically fell out of the truck.

His apartment wasn't nearly as fancy as Sean's, but it was a cozy two-room affair with comfortable, mismatched furniture and nature photos on the walls. Danesh led me right to the bathroom and turned on the shower. "Here's a towel," he said. "There should be a new toothbrush in the drawer, and use anything else you need. You want tea? Food?"

I shook my head, he left, and I stripped down and climbed into the shower. Even that seemed like a lot of effort, but the dried mud was starting to itch. Once I was in, the hot water revived me. Ten minutes later I stepped out and wrapped myself in a towel.

I found some aloe in the cabinet and was dabbing it on my scrapes when Danesh rapped on the door. "Want some clothes?"

Still wrapped in the towel, I opened the door and took the T-shirt and sweatpants he held. He winked. "Think you can keep these clean for more than twenty minutes?"

I laughed. "I'm not planning to do anything more exciting than sleep."

"The bed's ready. If you don't want anything else, climb on in. I'll be on the couch if you need me."

I thought about that as I dressed. It hardly seemed fair to take his bed. And besides—I didn't want to be alone. I was far from feeling frisky, but I suspected once the first exhaustion passed, my sleep would be restless. Too many things churned around in the back of my mind. If I'd suffered from posttraumatic stress disorder after the brief attack in Boston, what would this night's events do to me?

I stepped out to the living room, still not sure what I wanted. I noticed a pile of bedding on the couch but didn't see Danesh until sounds from the kitchen caught my attention. The kitchen was a narrow corridor separated from the living room by cabinets above and a counter below, with an open pass-through between. I could see Danesh's back, from his shoulders to his waist. He wasn't wearing a shirt.

Suddenly I wasn't in any hurry to get his attention. I stood for a minute, admiring the view. Muscles rippled in his shoulders and along his spine as he moved, like a Greek sculpture brought gloriously to life in warm, tanned flesh. I wanted to trace my fingers—or my mouth—along his spine. His hair hung loose over his shoulders, but I imagined sweeping it aside to nuzzle that delicious neck.

He turned, flashing me his chest and stomach. I leaned back against the wall with a sigh. I wanted to nibble my way over that feast of flesh. My body was telling me I was ready to get physical with a man. My mind and heart agreed—so long as it was this man.

He stepped out of the kitchen. A pair of baggy basketball shorts rode low on his hips and I had to drag my eyes up to his face. He smiled. "Did you decide you're hungry after all?"

Oh, I was getting hungry all right. I swallowed quickly before I started drooling—literally. "No. I wanted to talk about the sleeping arrangements."

He glanced at the bedding on the couch and then back at me. "If you're not comfortable here, we can still find a hotel."

I stepped closer. "It's not that. I'm afraid I'll have nightmares."

"Ah? After everything you've been through, that's not a surprise." He frowned, and I could tell he was trying to think of a solution. It was so cute.

I moved to him and slid my hands up his chest to rest on his shoulders. "I wondered if you might sleep next to me, in case I get scared."

His hands moved to my hips as he smiled down at me. "It's not a very big bed."

I said softly, "I've been sleeping on a twenty-inch-wide pad. I'm sure we can manage." I licked my lips and saw his gaze drop to my mouth.

He took a quick breath and said, "I would sure hate for you to have a nightmare and wake up all alone."

I leaned in and stretched up to whisper against his mouth. "Hold me tonight."

He crushed his mouth down on mine, dragging me tight against his body. We dove into the kiss like jumping off the high dive and plunging into deep, warm water. I melted against him until I didn't know where I ended and he began.

Some time later he loosened his grip, and we edged apart, gasping. He turned me toward the bedroom door and patted my hip. "You go on in, I have to turn off the lights and brush my teeth."

I strolled to the bedroom door with a coy glance over my shoulder. He watched me with the hungry eyes of a predator. I couldn't wait to be devoured.

I crawled into his bed and snuggled against the pillow, inhaling the faint, musky scent of him. What a night I'd had. It felt more like a week.

We still had too many questions unanswered, about Sean, about Jerry, about the future. I still had to sort out how I felt about some of the things that had happened, some of the things I'd done. But I knew one thing—I wanted Danesh. He excited me like no one ever had, and yet I felt safe with him. I needed the safety. I wanted the excitement. I'd found someone who offered both, and I wasn't about to give that up.

I lay with my eyes closed, my body heavy and aching with fatigue. My mind drifted. When Danesh came in a minute later, I tried to open my eyes, but could only manage a flutter of eyelids.

He slipped in next to me and put an arm around my waist. I heard him chuckle and say softly, "I guess I should have skipped brushing my teeth."

I turned to snuggle against him, murmured something incomprehensible even to me, and fell asleep.

Twenty-Eight

I woke once in the night. I'm not sure what I was dreaming, but I must have been thrashing or making some noise, because Danesh was pulling me closer with soothing whispers. My heart raced and I gasped for breath, but he stroked my hair and promised me everything was all right. I burrowed against him, my breathing slowed, and I drifted back to sleep.

When I woke again, light filtered through the curtains and I lay alone. I blinked groggily at the room until memories streamed back and I realized where I was and why. I yawned and stretched. My body ached and I felt like another five or ten hours of sleep wouldn't hurt me. But the smell of coffee sent my stomach rumbling, and I had to pee.

I sat up on the edge of the bed. The room seemed to sway a moment and then settle. I pushed myself up with a grunt and limped toward the bathroom, my leg muscles complaining and my sore feet a reminder of running around in sandals and then socks. My ankle felt stiff, but I could put my weight on it, and the pain hardly competed with all the other aches.

In the bathroom, I glanced at the shower and decided it was too much trouble. I was clean enough from last night, so I forced my hair into a ponytail, splashed water on my face, rewrapped my ankle, and called it good.

I smiled ruefully at my reflection. I hardly looked like the woman dressed up and ready for a night on the town—had it been only twelve or fifteen hours ago? At least Danesh had seen me much worse and didn't seem to mind. And if he could handle my aggressive come-on last night, followed by the quick if accidental turn down, he could probably handle anything I might throw at him.

If he was disappointed, I'd have to make it up to him. I smiled and headed out to find him.

He was making eggs in the kitchen. "Morning, sunshine." He pulled me close for a quick kiss and then went back to his work. "Coffee's ready. I heard you stirring so I started breakfast. I don't know about you, but I'm famished."

"Ravenous." I leaned closer and sniffed at the pan. It seemed to be some kind of omelet with hash browns, onions, and peppers. He grabbed a pile of shredded cheese and sprinkled that on top.

"Are you sure that's enough food?" I said. "Don't let my size fool you. I have a big appetite."

He laughed. "I have sausage broiling and toast in the toaster. I promise you won't leave here hungry."

I poured myself coffee with plenty of milk and sugar while Danesh set the table. Minutes later we were eating, and although we exchanged glances and smiles, I was too busy to talk.

Finally I leaned back with a sigh. "That was wonderful. You can make me breakfast any day." It was an offhand comment, but he studied me seriously. "What?" I asked.

"Maybe this is a good time to bring up the idea I had."

I raised my eyebrows and waited. He smiled shyly—I was getting to recognize every nuance of those subtle smiles—and went on. "I thought you might like to stay here for a couple of days. You need to recover from everything you went through yesterday, and I'll bet a bed and shower will help. Not to mention some good meals—which I'll happily supply."

I felt my smile growing and couldn't resist teasing. "Are you asking me to move in with you?"

He gave a nervous laugh, and I could see his

blush even through his tan. "I know it's early to talk about the future. I know you might be leaving in a few weeks."

He got up, paced across the room, came back, sat down. He looked up, took a deep breath. Looked down at the table and released it. I tried not to laugh.

When he finally met my eyes, his gaze pierced me and the laughter died. His husky voice sent an answering tremor through me. "I hope we can work out some way to be together, because you're the most amazing woman I've ever met, and I can't stand the thought of you walking out of my life."

He shook his head. "I wasn't going to bring all that up now. I don't want to add to your stress." As our glances held, I felt a little thrill of recognition—like I was looking at my soul mate.

I had wondered if I'd be able to let myself trust again. I realized it wasn't a simple matter of choice. I did trust Danesh. That didn't mean our relationship would be perfect or even easy—but I was ready to dive into life again, to take a chance on love and work my rear off to help us succeed.

He added softly, "I want to hold you at night and make the nightmares go away. I want to watch you work and take you dancing and learn everything about you."

I got up and slowly moved around the table, my gaze still locked to his. He pushed his chair back. Before he could stand, I put a hand on his shoulder and slid onto his lap, straddling him. "I think that's a very good idea. Is it too early to tell you that I've already started looking for jobs in this area? Even before I came out here—it's like some part of me knew."

His hands slid over my hips and he smiled, his dark eyes holding a kind of fire. I leaned in.

I paused with my lips an inch from his, savoring the tingle of anticipation, the warmth slowly spreading from my belly to my limbs. His smile filled with promises. He lifted a hand to stroke across my neck and around the back of my head. His fingers tangled in my hair and with gentle pressure he pulled me closer.

Our lips met with a sigh of welcome. We drifted into a languid, lazy kiss full of warmth and comfort. I could almost sense the universe spinning around us while his hands held me firmly grounded.

I gave a little murmur of pleasure and wriggled even closer. His hand still on my hip slipped under my T-shirt and stroked my back. I pressed against his chest, the feeling reminding me that I wasn't wearing a bra.

I nipped at his lip and then moved to feast on his delicious neck. His head fell back and he groaned.

His arms banded around me and he hauled me close. Desire flooded me, leaving me breathless and dizzy. I threaded my fingers in his hair and plundered his mouth.

I thought I would burst into flames.

"Oh yes," I panted.

The doorbell rang.

I jumped and we stared at each other. It took a good five seconds before my brain really processed what I'd heard. Danesh shook his head like a man waking from a dream.

We sat gasping for a moment. The doorbell rang again, a long demand that erased any hope the intruder would simply go away. I blew out a breath and then started laughing. "Is something wrong with my timing?"

Danesh stood, lifting me with him, and set me on my feet. He sighed and looked toward the door as the bell rang again. "I'd ignore it, but it could be the police. I told them we'd check in today, but they might be getting impatient."

I grimaced, hating the thought of facing uniforms again. They held bad associations, even if the police had always been on my side.

Danesh frowned. "Or it could be the press. If it is, I'll get rid of them. Stay out of sight for a minute."

The press. The omelet suddenly felt heavy in my

stomach. I did not want to do interviews, especially not now—before we'd sorted everything out about Jerry and learned what happened to Sean. I hurried to the bedroom as Danesh opened the front door.

I jolted when I recognized the voice from the next room. "Oh, Danny, what happened?" Maureen wailed. "They won't tell me anything, the police or the hospital, only that he's in serious condition and I can't even see him."

I felt a stab of guilt because I'd forgotten Maureen completely. I heard Danesh murmuring to her and decided to stay out of it. I didn't want to go over the story again, trying to hide Jerry's guilt. I didn't want to see Maureen's reaction, to know how much Jerry really meant to her—or didn't.

I glanced at the bed with a sigh. The tragedies of the real world had come crashing in, putting desire on hold. At least I had something to look forward to, and any lingering fears of intimacy had vanished. My mind had been so swamped with feelings for Danesh that no trauma from the past could get close.

I looked around Danesh's bedroom, trying to ignore the conversation in the next room. Bookshelves filled one wall. I scanned the titles and found German philosophy, English poetry, Native American folklore, *Zen and the Art of Motorcycle Maintenance*, and *The Tao of Pooh*.

One shelf held mysteries set in the Southwest by authors like J. Michael Orenduff, Steve Brewer, and Beth Groundwater, along with a set of "Learn Spanish" books and practice tapes.

National Geographic magazines filled one entire row. The bottom shelf featured oversized books—collections of photographs of the Southwest, photography instruction manuals, and three well-worn collections of *Calvin and Hobbes* cartoons.

I felt an odd sense of homecoming and smiled. I started to reach for one of the *Calvin and Hobbes* books, but the thought of home made me hesitate. Danesh had mentioned the press. Was this a big enough story to get picked up nationwide? Would my name be mentioned?

Even if it wasn't, any story about a woman archaeologist getting in trouble at Lost Valley would be enough to alarm my parents. I decided I'd better call home.

I wasn't sure where my phone was, but I found Danesh's and decided he wouldn't mind me using it. I dialed my parents' number and smiled as my mother answered on the second ring. "Hi, Mom."

"Kylie! How are you? Are you having a fun trip?"

"A lot has happened."

"Well, tell me! Anything fit for a mother's ears, at least."

Where should I start, and how could I tell it all? Memories tumbled through my mind—the canyon, Sean falling, the police station, falling asleep in Danesh's arms....

"I think I'm in love." I hadn't known I was going to say that. But I suddenly realized it was true and more important than anything else.

"Honey, that's wonderful! Tell me about him."

I tried to explain another person, to capture in words the nuances that made him special—his brilliant flash of smile, his annoying bossiness and deep compassion, his quirky humor and love of nature.

"Well, he sounds very nice," my mother said.

"And Mom, some stuff's been happening here, you might hear about it on the news, but don't worry. I'm all right." And I knew then that I was.

Twenty-Nine

Danesh tapped on the half-open door. "We're going to the hospital. Like to come?"

Maureen stood behind him, her eyes huge and shiny but her makeup somehow still intact. She stared at me, but I'm not sure she really saw me. I nodded and went to join them. Maureen wasn't the only one who wanted answers.

Danesh said, "After that, we can head out to the park. You can pick up your things, and I should check in at the office. Given the circumstances, we're closing for the day, but I left the visitors center unlocked last night so the search team could use it as a base."

He led us outside, where a little red sports car was parked at a crazy angle to the curb. Maureen pulled out her keys. Danesh glanced at her shaking hands and took the keys from her. "Kylie, do you want to drive Maureen's car and follow me, or do you feel comfortable driving the truck?"

I wasn't sure what I would say to Maureen during the drive, but I wasn't confident with the truck in traffic. I took the keys.

No need to worry about making conversation. Maureen was too distracted even to comment on the fact that I'd spent the night with Danesh. She stared out the window, silent except for an occasional short, jerky breath.

Danesh turned into a parking lot a few minutes later. If it weren't for the signs, I wouldn't have recognized it as a hospital, since the low building had little in common with the mammoth complexes I knew in Boston.

Maureen jumped out and ran for the building, not even bothering to close her door properly. I took care of that and went in with Danesh. We found Maureen at the counter, babbling and gesturing wildly. The pretty young woman behind the counter gazed at her complacently.

The receptionist turned to Danesh. "Hey sweetie, how's the hero?" Sweetie? And I couldn't help noticing her long, glossy brown hair and great figure.

He put his arm around me. "I don't know, you'll have to ask Kylie. Kylie, my cousin Alice."

"Oh." I blinked at her as she turned her curious gaze on me. "Pleased to meet you." A cousin was all right.

Then I processed the rest of their conversation. Hero? I didn't feel like a hero. I didn't even know yet if I was a murderer. Not murderer, I reminded myself—it was self-defense. But still, I'd caused someone's death. Manslaughterer, maybe.

"Please, can I see Jerry?" Maureen wailed.

"I'll check," Alice said. She headed down the hallway.

"But if she can see him, why can't I see him?" Maureen demanded.

Danesh took her arm and steered her toward the waiting area. "She works here. Be patient." He nudged Maureen into a chair.

I sat nearby and stared at the posters on the wall without really seeing them. Would I ever be able to enter a police station or hospital again without triggering unpleasant memories? I wanted to go to Danesh, to ask him to hold me, but Maureen needed him more than I did.

I breathed deeply and started doing my grounding exercises. Surely I'd proven one thing last night—that I could keep going when the going got tough. I hadn't forgotten the blind panic that sent me climbing up to the Castle. And trying to explain to the police the logic behind that had not been easy, since I now saw there wasn't any. Still, for every stupid situation I'd gotten myself into, I'd gotten myself out again. No way was I a hero, but I'd done something. I'd shown up. I could hold onto that.

Alice came back a minute later. "You can see him, but only one at a time." As Maureen started to rise, Alice gestured to Danesh and added, "He wants to see you first."

Maureen froze halfway to her feet. "Not ... not me?"

Danesh patted her shoulder. "I'm sure he wants to see you, too. I'll only be a minute. Then he'll be all yours."

Maureen settled back in her chair with a little whimper and stared after Danesh as he followed Alice down the hall. She hardly seemed aware of me.

I hoped Jerry wouldn't ask to see me. What could I say to him? You nearly got me killed, you made me hurt people, maybe kill one, but it's all right? It wasn't all right, and I didn't want to face any of the criminals involved.

But Jerry was in the hospital, seriously injured. Two men were in jail, facing long sentences. Sean was probably dead. I was healthy except for bruises and blisters that would heal in a few days. I was free, and now I had Danesh and a future. I was clearly the winner, if there was such a thing. Maybe that didn't make up for the terror that would still haunt me, but I could count my blessings.

I moved to the chair next to Maureen and spoke gently. "I'm sure he'll be all right. He must be conscious if he asked for Danesh."

She turned tear-filled eyes on me. "I love him," she whispered. "I really do love him, and I've been so hard on him ... pushing him to get a better job, nagging him about money. I might have lost him last night. I've been worrying about how well we're going to live, when we should just be living. We should be starting a family. He's a good man and he'll be a good father. I don't want to waste any more time."

She put her hand over her mouth and started crying. I patted her arm awkwardly and mumbled something meaningless.

A minute later, Maureen jumped up and raced for the hallway. Alice turned back with her while Danesh joined me. He sat with a sigh. "Jerry wanted me to apologize. He feels terrible that he put you in danger. He swears he didn't mean to—you scared him when you came in with that story of seeing Sean, and he panicked. He called Sean to warn him, but he thought they'd run, not come back."

"But how did he get involved in the first place?"

"He stumbled on Sean one night doing something suspicious. Sean spun a story about being an undercover agent. Said Jerry would be helping the FBI if he played along and acted as a lookout."

I frowned. "And he believed it? Did he even ask for ID?"

"Jerry admits that he suspected Sean might be lying. But Sean offered money ... Jerry was afraid he'd lose Maureen if he didn't marry her soon, and she's the kind of woman who expects a big flashy ring, things like that. Sean offered a thousand dollars for every meeting where Jerry acted as lookout and bonuses for providing information in between. It's been going on for two months, long enough to buy Maureen that ring. Jerry convinced himself that it didn't matter too much."

He shrugged and shook his head. "The whole thing is ludicrous. I can't understand why Sean went to all that trouble. Why didn't he find someplace else after Jerry saw him? Why choose that location in the first place? It's ridiculously complicated."

I remembered something one of the criminals had said out in the ruins about Sean trying to be clever. "I think it was a game to him. Using Jerry, trying to pull one over on me, flirting with danger by using someplace remote and yet still too public. He was playing at being some kind of criminal mastermind. It wasn't sensible, but it must have given him a thrill to manipulate people and take risks. Like some role-playing video game brought to life."

"Yeah, maybe. That game's over, anyway."

I shifted uncomfortably in the plastic chair. "And as foolish as it may look now, he almost got away with it. If I hadn't happened along at exactly the wrong moment, and been stupid enough to investigate, he could have pulled it off."

He reached over and took my hand, linking his fingers through mine. We sat silently. The hospital was strangely peaceful—no sirens blared as ambulances pulled up, no urgent announcements came over loudspeakers. Any drama was tucked away quietly in private rooms.

Finally I said, "I thought they were a strange couple. But she really cares. More about him than the money, I mean. How do you think she'll feel if she finds out what he did?"

Danesh chuckled. "Knowing Maureen, she'll be flattered. She'll say he's finally showing some initiative."

He shifted in his chair to face me and put his hands on my arms. "Kylie, it's up to you. I still don't want to say anything about Jerry to the police. I think he'll tell them himself, but if they believe he was tricked into it, he should get off." He ran his hands up my arms and cupped my face. "But you could have died last night. If you want to insist on justice, I'll stand by you."

I shook my head. "I don't see the point in ruining more lives. I don't know if I can forgive and forget, but I'll try to at least forgive." I started to smile. "Although I'm not convinced we're doing him a great favor. Maureen is talking about starting a family right away."

Danesh pulled me close and squeezed, laughing. "He's on his own. I'll face the police, but I'm not taking on Maureen."

He leaned back and stretched. "Well, Maureen will probably be a while, and she has her own car. Let's head out to the canyon. I'd like to know what's happened since we left."

Thirty

Half an hour later we passed a police car at the park entrance, turning tourists away. Ten minutes after that, we pulled up beside a police car in the visitors center parking lot. I suppressed a shiver and told myself it wasn't the police's fault that I kept running into them in unpleasant circumstances. They were a trigger for my anxiety, but one I could overcome.

I lowered myself gingerly from the truck. Thick socks and my tennis shoes cushioned my sore feet, but my muscles ached. I held the open door for balance as I turned stiffly to shut the door. Something on the floor of the cab caught my eye.

My pepper spray.

I stared at it. How had it gotten—?

I groaned. It must have fallen out of my pack when I got my phone to call the police. I hadn't spotted it on the dark floor. Oh well, the squash had worked, maybe even better since the effects lasted longer. I put the spray back in my backpack, which was also still in the car, and trailed Danesh into the office.

Danesh hailed a man in the back room by name. He and Danesh leaned over the map on the coffee table while they talked.

"No sign of the missing man yet, dead or alive," the officer said. "We've done a pretty thorough search of the whole canyon, for one mile upstream and two down. I'm glad you're here. We want to get up into some of the ruins in case he's hiding, but a couple of them are hard to access."

"I can help you with that," Danesh said. "I gather he's pretty familiar with the site."

"If he drowned, he could be miles downriver, and the area isn't exactly easy to search. We've called out a rafting team. They should be here in an hour. That's the most likely scenario, but we don't want to take any chances."

I shuddered and stared at a poster on the wall. I recognized the high cliffs of Yosemite towering over dark green forests and cool water. I wondered if that had been Jerry's poster, reflecting a dream of someplace he thought would be better.

"That guy couldn't have been the ringleader, surely," Danesh said.

"No, just a local contact," the police officer replied. "We picked up a drug lord a few months ago, and we think this man Sean stepped in to fill the gap. The stuff is coming in from the south. The two we have in custody—the older one's American, but he's lived in Belize for twenty years. We have his prints on file. We're still trying to identify the younger man, but he may be from Central America."

I paced, hugging myself to ward off a chill. I'd heard enough. I touched Danesh's shoulder and said, "I'm going to my campsite."

He caught my hand. "Wait a minute." He spoke to the officer. "What about the campsite? Is it safe?"

"We did a thorough sweep, and we warned everyone staying there. We have someone checking cars on the way out, too, in case he decides to try hitching a ride."

Danesh's thumb rubbed over my knuckles, and he looked up at me. "All right. Can you check on the Wests? I want to make sure they don't need anything, and it looks like I could be busy here for a while."

I nodded and withdrew, hoping Danesh hadn't noticed the way my pulse jumped when they started talking about the safety of the campground. It hadn't occurred to me that Sean—if he were even alive—might have made it back up here, but now the shady path through the woods looked ominous. I got my pepper spray, but even armed, I decided to take the longer and busier route and headed for the canyon rim.

When I reached the rim, I paused and gazed out over the canyon. I barely recognized the nightmare world of the night before. The Castle stood beautiful, ancient, and mysterious, the blocks glowing a warm red against the blue sky. The sun shone down, bright and cheerful, warm on my face. I'd want to change from sweats to shorts soon.

The depths of the canyon stretched out below me, still cool in the shade. I caught glimpses of the river and trembled at the thought of Sean's body tumbling through the water for miles.

I concentrated on my breathing and forced myself to gaze down. I would not allow the horrors of the previous night to ruin this place for me. It meant so much more than the folly and cruelty of a few men.

If I avoided every place where I'd had a bad experience, my world would keep shrinking. I'd lose not only those places, but the opportunities—and the people—that came with them.

I still had work to do here, and I would do it. I had something special with Danesh, and I would explore it.

But I wondered how long it would be before they found Sean. He couldn't have survived without serious injury, but I hoped he was alive, for the sake of my conscience. I didn't need that particular ghost haunting my memories.

I nodded to a few tourists as I walked along the rim before turning down the path to the campground. Birds sang in the trees, and I flinched only a little when something small rustled in a bush. I spotted the Wests as I neared their campsite and found myself smiling before I was even close enough to wave.

"Kylie!" Lily lumbered to her feet and embraced me. "Have you been getting into trouble again?"

I tucked the pepper spray in my pocket and met her embrace. "Something like that."

She insisted on sending Robert into the RV for fresh cups of coffee and a plate of cookies. I sat and gave them a quick version of the night's activities.

Lily shook her head over Sean. "Nice-looking young man like that. I guess you never can tell. He seemed so friendly when he stopped by to visit the other day, but I guess he had ulterior motives."

"Yeah, he had a lot of them."

She eyed me closely. "You disappointed?"

I felt myself blushing. "Actually ... I seem to be dating Danesh now."

She beamed. "Well! You couldn't do better than that."

"Do you know him well?" I asked.

"Sure, he stops by two, three times a week at least. Has lunch with us, makes sure everything is all right."

Robert nodded. "Good fellow. Helped me with the septic system."

I deduced that this had something to do with the RV. It was nice to know Danesh had mechanical skills, along with everything else he offered. But I decided to change the subject before it got more personal. "How are Amanda and the kids?"

"Things are progressing," Lily said. "We got them into a shelter and the boys are enjoying the other kids. I'll keep an eye on her, but she has support in town now, and I missed Robert."

She leaned toward him, and I had a feeling that his hand, out of sight under the table, had reached for her leg. The tender look they exchanged showed how much they cared for each other, and I had already seen how they worked as a team. I had a sudden vision of Danesh and myself, in our sixties, traveling the country by RV and occasionally meddling helpfully in other people's lives.

I smiled, finished my cookie, and rose. "I'm going to go pack up my things. I'm staying in town for a few days." I decided not to mention exactly where I was staying, but Lily gave me a knowing look. I added, "I'll still be out here working most days, so I'll see you."

"You come by for lunch any time," Lily said. "You and your young man."

I walked away chuckling.

I strolled through the woods, taking my time. I saw a few cars and tents, but no people. Of course, the police were turning away everyone who didn't have legitimate business. Those who'd camped overnight must be taking advantage of the beautiful morning to get out and see the site. Or else, people being what they were, they were watching the police search.

I wondered how long Danesh would need. I wasn't even going to pretend that I would get work done that day. Besides the obvious advantage to staying out of the canyon until they found Sean, my muscles seemed to stiffen up every time I sat for a few minutes. This was a day to take things easy—and I was getting hungry again. I probably still had calories to make up from the night before.

I stopped by my picnic table and surveyed the campsite. Footprints crisscrossed the ground. At least two and maybe three different people had been there, pausing at the car and the tent. I put a hand to my chest and rubbed where my heart seemed too close to the surface.

"It's only from the police search," I muttered. I tried not to picture strange men peering into my tent and car. At least I hadn't been there to be startled and frightened. I wondered how other campers had reacted to the disturbance last night.

I definitely needed to get away for a day or two. I might as well pack up everything, load the car, and take it into town. In the future, I could ride in with Danesh, or maybe borrow the truck.

The tent still had a few damp spots from the rain but seemed to be drying quickly. I retrieved my food from the critter-proof metal box the site provided and packed it into the box in my trunk, except for an apple, which I ate.

I finished my snack and stood looking at the tent while the breeze rustled in the trees and a bird chirped somewhere nearby. I was dawdling. The damp spots on the rain fly had almost faded. By the time I got my sleeping bag into the stuff sack, the foam pad rolled up, and everything retrieved from the side pockets, the tent would be dry. Yet I couldn't quite bring myself to touch it.

I knew the site had been searched, I knew Sean was most likely miles away, but somehow "what if?" played in my brain. I pictured unzipping the tent and seeing Sean glaring out at me.

I shook my head. I couldn't go running back to Danesh and ask him to unzip my tent for me. He had called me a hero not two hours before. Heroes didn't run and hide because of foolish fears, and sensible, independent, grown-up women didn't make the men do all the dirty work.

They didn't take unnecessary chances, either. But I could easily find out whether anyone was inside the tent. I crouched at the corner and yanked out the thin metal stake holding the tent into the ground. I moved to the one along the side and then the one at the back corner. I remembered how hard I'd had to pound to get those six-inch pieces of metal, no thicker than a coat hanger, into the dry ground. They slid out easily.

I grabbed the side of the tent and stood, lifting the tent with me. I heard and felt my sleeping bag and pad slide to the other side. No one could be inside, or a heavy body would have held down the tent.

I dropped the tent, moved to the front, and unzipped the zipper. I knelt with my knees inside the tent but my feet still out, so I wouldn't track in mud. I needed to put away the tent stakes first, before I lost track of them.

I dragged my sleeping bag and pad back to the middle of the tent and reached for the built-in storage bag hanging from the side of the tent, where I'd stashed the nylon stuff sacks that held the tent parts. I had to lean on my right elbow and stretch to reach. My fingers caught the edge of the hanging bag, and I fished around inside, plucking at the stuff sacks.

A shadow passed over the tent, breaking up the light that poured through the blue nylon. I sensed motion behind me.

I dropped the stuff sacks and shifted my weight back on my knees. Before I could turn, something slammed against my back. I sprawled on my stomach, my face buried in my sleeping bag. A heavy weight pressed down on me.

I recognized Sean's voice even though it sounded hoarse and raw. "It's about time."

Thirty-One

I couldn't move. I couldn't breathe. Pressure weighed me down as my heart thundered, and my mouth gasped futilely against the suffocating fabric. My mind swirled, edging toward unconsciousness.

The pressure eased. I raised my head enough to drag in a breath.

Before I could do more, he was rolling me over. The world wobbled crazily and then settled down into one sight, one feeling: Sean staring down at me from inches away, his body heavy on top of mine.

"Do you know what this night has been like?" he muttered.

His words barely penetrated. His body, all too real and solid, pinned me down.

"That river nearly killed me. Then I had to drag myself back up here—crawling up that slope! And then I find the police everywhere. I barely got across the path without them seeing me. I've been hiding in the woods for hours."

His eyes jerked around, seeing not me but his memories. Mud streaked his face, and a lump on his forehead had trickled blood.

I squeezed my eyes shut tight, as if that would make him go away. This couldn't be real. It couldn't be. It couldn't be. I prayed to wake up, for the nightmare to go away.

"You got me into this," Sean hissed. "So you can help get me out. You're going to drive me out of here. They'll let you past. And if you try anything ..." He jerked his body so it slammed harder against mine, shoving the last of the air out of my lungs and sending pain shooting through my ribs.

I whimpered like a wounded animal. Sean eased back enough so I could breathe again, but the cry echoed in my mind. I seemed to observe it from far away. Had I really made that sound? Was that wounded animal me?

The thought grounded me. My mind wanted to slip away, to go to some other, safer place, until this was all over. But I couldn't let it.

I pulled air into my lungs and noticed how my tight throat burned. Sean was still talking, but I ignored his words and focused on my body's sensations. As much as I might hate the feel of Sean's weight pressing down on me, it was real, it was now. I had to stay with the moment or risk being even more helpless. If I let my mind slip away, I didn't know when I might get it back.

But I couldn't shift Sean's weight. I couldn't push him away. I couldn't run. I couldn't even scream, because I didn't have enough air in my lungs. He must be hurt, but he still held me helpless.

I had to fight the panic. I grabbed onto one of the exercises my counselor had given me to fight disassociation. With my eyes still closed, I focused on my hand, only my hand. That was less overwhelming than acknowledging all the pain and fear coursing through my body.

My left hand was out to the side, with Sean's arm leaning hard against my forearm. My left hand was going numb. Numb wasn't good. Numb was dangerous.

I shook away the thought. Focus! Find one thing and hold onto it.

My right arm was stretched above my head. I felt softness around my hand. The fuzzy flannel lining of my sleeping bag. When Sean had flipped me over, my hand must have gotten buried in the bag.

But my hand hurt. I was making a fist, clenching so hard the muscles ached. I told myself to relax that hand. It took a moment, but finally the muscles twitched. Something shifted in my hand. The thin metal tent stakes, now warm against my palm.

Sean shifted his body off of me, and I opened my eyes to see what he was doing. He kept one shin crossed over my thighs, holding me down, and grabbed my left shoulder. "When I move my leg, you get up slowly," he said. "You make a sound and I'll hit you so hard you'll never make a sound again. We're going to your car, nice and easy, and then we're getting out of here."

I studied him quickly, needing to know exactly what I had to deal with. He held his other arm close to his stomach, with the fingers loosely curled. He must have hurt his arm or wrist.

He hadn't said anything about the gun. If he had it, surely he'd be pointing it at me. He must have lost it when he fell.

He'd already shown that he didn't need the gun to subdue me. But if I could get away, he might not be able to catch me. Not if he was hurt badly enough, and he'd talked about crawling up the slope, not running. He didn't have a weapon, besides his body.

And I did.

I flexed my hand and felt the thin metal spikes. Sean glared down at me, maybe trying to make sure I was properly frightened. I stared at him with wide eyes, trying not to let my gaze flicker while my mind raced. Where to hit him? When? He was blocking my exit now, but once I pulled my hand out from the sleeping bag, he might see the stakes. I'd lose the surprise.

Sean leaned out the entrance to look around, his hand still gripping my shoulder hard enough to grind the bones together and his leg still pinning mine. He pulled on my shoulder and growled, "Get up."

As I sat up, I slid my hand out from the sleeping bag and glanced down to make sure the stakes were pointing in the right direction. It wouldn't do much good to stab him with the rounded loops at the tops.

The pointed ends were sticking out from the pinky side of my hand, so I would need to swing my arm down at him.

Sean turned back toward me.

I swung my arm up and stabbed toward his cheek. He jerked back and raised his free hand to catch at my forearm. That slowed my blow and the metal stakes scratched down his cheek, leaving a red line.

And yet Sean howled and fell back. I squirmed out from under his leg and crawled past him. As I glanced at him, I saw he was holding his wrist, not his face. The stakes had done little damage, but he'd blocked me with his injured wrist, and that had apparently hurt.

I stumbled to my feet outside the tent. Between the adrenaline and the sore muscles, I staggered against the picnic table before I got myself under control. Then I found my footing and raced toward the visitors center, screaming for help.

Thirty-Two

Could they hear me all the way over at the visitors center? Would Sean follow me or take off in the other direction?

With my mind racing over these questions, I forgot about my own injury. I got to the trees at the edge of my campsite and then my ankle gave out.

I crashed to the ground, my cries for help cut off by a grunt. I rolled over and sat up, looking back at Sean. He was on his knees in the tent doorway. He grabbed the external tent frame and pulled himself up, but the poles slumped under his weight and he swayed, flailing his free arm for balance. He swore and pushed off toward me, limping badly.

Hysterical laughter bubbled in my chest. The lame chasing the lame.

But that didn't mean I wanted him to catch me. I grabbed a small juniper beside me for balance as I scrambled to my feet. I knew I'd hurt my ankle worse if I kept running on it, but surely I could outpace Sean in his present state.

Movement caught my eye at the far side of the clearing—the Wests hurrying toward us.

Sean had almost reached me. He must have noticed my attention shift, because he glanced back at the Wests. He turned to me and said, "Give me your car keys and I'll go. You don't want anyone else hurt."

No, I didn't. Even injured, Sean might prove a threat to the elderly couple. He might get a hostage and drag this out longer. But I didn't trust him to take the keys and leave. He had to know he'd be better off with a hostage.

He lunged at me. I felt his arm brush past my hair as I dropped to the ground.

I grabbed a dead branch a couple of feet long. Sean took a step back but swayed on unsteady legs. I rose up on my knees and swung the branch at the leg he was favoring.

The thwack of the branch hitting his knee was almost drowned out by the loud pop of something dislocating. Sean shrieked and toppled like a bowling pin.

Robert and Lily crossed the clearing and stared down at him. I stayed on my knees, panting, still gripping the branch.

"He looks the worse for wear." Lily sounded satisfied. "Did you do all that to him?"

"It's less than he deserved," Robert said.

Sean groaned and pushed himself up to sitting. He looked like a wild animal, ready to fight for survival. Would I have to hit him again?

I suddenly remembered the pepper spray. Oh, good grief, I might as well throw the stupid stuff away if I wasn't going to use it when I needed it.

What the heck. I pulled it out of my pocket. "Stand back," I told Lily and Robert. Sean's eyes widened as I held up the pepper spray. Before he could duck, I set it off. His scream was satisfying.

I heard footsteps coming up behind me, but I didn't look back. Someone skidded to a stop beside me and crouched. An arm went around me.

Another person pushed into the clearing, a policeman with gun drawn. "What's happening here?" he asked. "Is this the fugitive?"

Lily answered him as Sean writhed on the ground. I started to tremble and finally dropped the spray. Danesh pulled me close. "Are you all right?"

I leaned against him, burying my face in his shoulder. He held me as I shook. I inhaled the scent of him and focused on the feel of his arms around me. A wisp of his hair tickled my forehead. This moment was real, now. I could hold on to this.

The police officer spoke into a radio and then started to read Sean his rights. Danesh whispered, "It's all over now. You're safe."

Yes. I'd done my part. Someone else could take over now. I took a deep breath and blew it out. Sean wasn't dead, which was good for my conscience. He was captured, which was good for society. And I had proven yet again that I could keep going, no matter how tough the going got. Maybe my plans didn't always play out like I'd hoped, but I had been able to act. And I would be able to go forward, without the past haunting me.

Danesh shifted to sit cross-legged and pulled me into his lap. I snuggled against him with a sigh. His arms tightened around me, but I felt him tremble. "You scared me," he murmured. "We were at the rim when we heard that scream ... But I should've known you'd be taking care of things." He rubbed his cheek against mine. "Have I mentioned you're amazing?"

I leaned back enough to look into his face and smiled. "Sometimes I amaze even myself."

"What do you need now? What do you want?"

I thought for a minute. "A couple of aspirin for my ankle. An enormous lunch. And then ..." I leaned in, brushing my cheek against his. I thought we could make it. I knew now I had the strength to work through the hard times. I couldn't be perfect. I might not always be strong enough to succeed in the short term. But I thought I could make it for the long haul.

I whispered in his ear. "And then I think I'd like to spend the rest of the afternoon in bed."

He pressed a kiss to my neck. "You've certainly earned your rest." He paused as I nibbled his earlobe. "You did mean you'd spend the afternoon resting, right?"

I chuckled. "Maybe some of that, too."

Dear Readers,

If you enjoyed these adventures, please leave a review! Reviews help authors find an audience, and they help readers find great books. To review, visit my Amazon page. Even a few lines help readers find books.

The setting for Whispers in the Dark was inspired by a visit to Hovenweep National Monument, on the Utah-Colorado border in the Four Corners area. I gave my setting a fictional name because I wanted the freedom to change details of the park and surrounding towns. Hovenweep is a Ute Indian word meaning "deserted valley," so I chose to name my fictional site Lost Valley.

If you get the chance, try to visit Hovenweep or one of the other Ancestral Pueblo cultural sites in the Southwest, such as Chaco Culture National Historical Park (Chaco Canyon) or Mesa Verde National Park. At Hovenweep, you'll see many of the ruins described in this story, though names and details may be different.

I hope you'll look for my other books. My latest project is a sweet romance series set around a cat café. Sign up for my newsletter at https://sendfox.com/lp/1g5nx3 and get a free novella set in the world of the Furrever Friends cat café, plus recipes mentioned in the cat café novels.

You can also visit my website at www.krisbock.com, or follow me on Amazon (go to my author page and click on the "Follow" button to the left) or BookBub (button in the upper right corner) if you only want New Release Alerts.

Kris Bock

Ordinary Women, Extraordinary Adventures

Kris Bock writes action-packed romantic suspense, often involving outdoor adventures and Southwestern landscapes. Her stories will interest fans of Terry Odell, Mary Stewart, Lillian Stewart Carl, and Barbara Michaels. Books include *The Mad Monk's Treasure, The Dead Man's Treasure, Counterfeits, What We Found,* and *Whispers in the Dark.* Read excerpts at www.krisbock.com or visit her Amazon page.

Sign up for the Kris Bock newsletter: http://eepurl.com/5Dd_f. for new releases and special offers.

Cover designed by the late **Rollin Thomas**, who was an award-winning illustrator, author, designer, and educator. The cover includes photographs by Anette Romanenko, John Sfondilias, George Burba, and T1000s, from Dreamstime.

The Furrever Friends Sweet Romance series features the workers and customers at a small-town cat café, and the adorable cats and kittens looking for their forever homes. Each book is a complete story with a happy ending for one couple (and maybe more than one rescued cat). These sweet romances will leave you with the warm, fuzzy feeling of cuddling a purring cat.

Coffee and Crushes at the Cat Café: a Furrever Friends Sweet Romance

What do you do when you meet the guy of your dreams? Set him up with your sister, of course.

Kari doesn't have time for love when she's opening her new cat café. She's busy hiring employees, fighting with the health inspector – oh, and welcoming 16 shelter cats. She's doing this for the cats, the community, and her family. The café will give her sister, Marley, a job worthy of her baking skills.

Then a tattooed military vet wanders in claiming he's a master baker. Surely Marley will fall for a guy this sweet, this sexy, this tasty.

Colin has other ideas. It's Kari who makes him want to turn up the heat. But he's spent the last two years recovering from physical and psychological wounds. Is he really ready for a relationship? He's not even sure he should commit to Samson, the sweet Siamese cat who steals his heart.

What We Found

22-year-old Audra Needham is back in her small New Mexico hometown. She simply wants to fit in, work hard, and help her younger brother. Going for a walk in the woods with her former crush, Jay, is a harmless distraction.

Until they stumble on a body.

Jay, who has secrets of his own to protect, insists they walk away and keep quiet. But Audra can't forget what she's seen. The woman deserves to be found, and her story deserves to be told.

More than one person isn't happy about Audra bringing a crime to life. The dead woman was murdered, and Audra could be next on the vengeful killer's list. She'll have to stand up for herself in order to stand up for the murder victim. It's a risk, and so is reaching out to the mysterious young man who works with deadly birds of prey. With her 12-year-old brother determined to play detective, and romance budding in the last place she expected, Audra learns that some risks are worth taking – no matter the danger, to her body or her heart.

Praise for *What We Found*:

"Another action-packed suspense novel by Kris Bock, perhaps her best to date. The author weaves an intriguing tale with appealing characters. Watching Audra, the main character, evolve into an emotionally-mature and independent young woman is gratifying."

"This book had me guessing to the end. Well written characters drive the story. Good romance. Exceptional and believable plot twists and turns. I loved it!"

"This is a nonstop suspense. Love the characters and how real they seem with every episode played out. This is a love story and suspense all in one."

Counterfeits

Painter Jenny Kinley has spent the last decade struggling in the New York art world. Her grandmother's sudden death brings her home to New Mexico, but inheriting the children's art camp her grandmother ran is more of a burden than a gift. How can she give up her lifelong dreams of showing her work in galleries and museums?

Rob Caruso, the camp cook and all-around handyman, would be happy to run the camp with Jenny. Dare he even dream of that, when his past holds dark secrets that he can never share? When Jenny's father reappears after a decade-long absence, only Rob knows where he's been and what danger he's brought with him.

Jenny and Rob face midnight break-ins and make desperate escapes, but the biggest danger may come from the secrets that don't want to stay buried. In the end, they must decide whether their dreams will bring them together or force them apart.

Praise for *Counterfeits*:

"*Counterfeits* is the kind of romantic suspense novel I have enjoyed since I first read Mary Stewart's *Moonspinners*, and Kris Bock used all the things I love about this genre. Appealing lead characters, careful development of the mysterious danger facing one or both of those characters, a great location that is virtually a character on its own, interesting secondary characters who might or might not be involved or threatened, and many surprises building up to the climax." 5 Stars – Roberta at Sensuous Reviews blog

"Counterfeits actually kept me guessing! ... I love when a writer manages to do that to me. Grab *Counterfeits* and keep trying to guess. Be surprised like I was." – Rochelle Weber, Roses & Thorns Reviews

The Mad Monk's Treasure

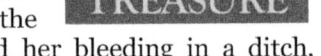

The lost Victorio Peak treasure is the stuff of legends—a heretic Spanish priest's gold mine, made richer by the spoils of bandits and an Apache raider. When Erin, a quiet history professor, uncovers a clue that may pinpoint the lost treasure cave, she prepares for adventure.

But when a hit and run driver nearly kills her, she realizes she's not the only one after the treasure. And is Drew, the handsome helicopter pilot who found her bleeding in a ditch, really a hero, or one of the enemy?

Erin isn't sure she can trust Drew with her heart, but she'll need his help to track down the treasure. She heads into the New Mexico wilderness with her brainy best friend Camie and a feisty orange cat. The wilderness holds its own dangers, from wild animals to sudden storms. Plus, the sinister men hunting Erin are determined to follow her all the way to the treasure, no matter where the twisted trail leads.

Erin won't give up an important historical find without a fight, but is she ready to risk her life—and her heart?

[*The Mad Monk's Treasure* was originally published as *Rattled*.]

Praise for *The Mad Monk's Treasure*:

"This book kept me turning its pages until I finished it. The action never stopped and I just had to know what happened next. I really cared what happened to the heroine. I loved the sexy helicopter pilot and enjoyed the romance even when I was on the edge of my chair with the action. It was adventure and romance at its best."

"The story has it all – action, romance, danger, intrigue, lost treasure, not to mention a sizzling relationship …"

"[It] kept me on the edge of my chair. It's one of those books I couldn't put down."

The Dead Man's Treasure

Rebecca Westin is shocked to learn the grandfather she never knew has left her a bona fide buried treasure – but only if she can decipher a complex series of clues leading to it. The hunt would be challenging enough without interference from her half-siblings, who are determined to find the treasure first and keep it for themselves. Good thing Rebecca has recruited some help.

Sam is determined to show Rebecca that a desert adventure can be sexy and fun. But there's a treacherous wildcard in the mix, a man willing to do anything to get that treasure – and revenge.

Action and romance combine in this lively Southwestern adventure, complete with riddles the reader is invited to solve to identify historical and cultural sites around New Mexico. See the "Books" page of my website for a printable list of the clues and recipes from the book.

"*The Dead Man's Treasure* is fast-paced and a perfect read for the weekend. I highly recommend this one."

"I can't say enough how much I loved this book! It has mystery, adventure, danger, romance, and above it all family remains a huge theme."

The Mad Monk's Treasure is the first of the Southwest Treasure Hunters novels. *The Dead Man's Treasure* is book 2 and *The Skeleton Canyon Treasure* is book 3. Each novel stands alone and is complete, with no cliffhangers. This series mixes action and adventure with romance. The stories explore the Southwest, especially New Mexico.

Ms. Bock also writes for young people as **Chris Eboch**. Her novels are appropriate for ages nine and up.

The Eyes of Pharaoh is a mystery set in ancient Egypt. This story of drama and intrigue brings an ancient world to life as three friends investigate a plot against the Pharaoh.

In *The Well of Sacrifice*, a Mayan girl in ninth-century Guatemala rebels against the High Priest who sacrifices anyone challenging his power.

Kirkus Reviews said, "[An] engrossing first novel.... Eboch crafts an exciting narrative with a richly textured depiction of ancient Mayan society.... The novel shines not only for a faithful recreation of an unfamiliar, ancient world, but also for the introduction of a brave, likable and determined heroine."

The Genie's Gift is a lighthearted action novel that draws on the mythology of The Arabian Nights. Shy and timid Anise determines to find the Genie Shakayak and claim the Gift of Sweet Speech. But the way is barred by a series of challenges, both ordinary and magical. How will Anise get past a vicious she-ghoul, a sorceress who turns people to stone, and mysterious sea monsters, when she can't even speak in front of strangers?

The Haunted series follows a brother and sister who travel with their parents' ghost hunter TV show and try to help the ghosts.

In *The Ghost on the Stairs*, an 1880s ghost bride haunts a Colorado hotel, waiting for her missing husband to return.

The Riverboat Phantom features a steamboat pilot still trying to prevent a long-ago disaster. In *The Knight in the Shadows*, a Renaissance French squire protects a sword on display at a New York City museum.

During *The Ghost Miner's Treasure*, Jon and Tania help a dead man find his lost gold mine—but they're not the only ones looking for it.

Bandits Peak

While hiking in the mountains, Jesse meets a strange trio. He befriends Maria, but he's suspicious of the men with her. Still, charmed by Maria, Jesse promises not to tell anyone that he met them. But his new friends have deadly secrets, and Jesse uncovers them. It will take all his wilderness skills, and all his courage, to survive.

Readers who enjoyed Gary Paulsen's *Hatchet* will love *Bandits Peak*. This heart-pounding adventure tale is full of danger and excitement.

Learn more or read excerpts at www.chriseboch.com.

All rights reserved. For information about permission to reproduce selections from this book, contact the author through her website at www.krisbock.com.

This is a work of fiction. Names, characters, places, and incidents are the product of the author's imagination. Any resemblance to actual persons, living or dead, is entirely coincidental.

Printed in Great Britain
by Amazon